'I'm going to the men's department," Bunny said. "Let's see, about a size fifteen shirt, twenty-eight long pants, nine narrow shoes, shorts and undershirts size small—"

"You think I'm wearing men's shorts?" Harriet interrupted, her voice rising.

"Don't worry, I'll pick out pastel shades. The new jockey shorts are very pretty," she joked.

After Bunny left, Harriet walked to the mirror and stared at herself. With the initial shock worn off, she looked quizzically at this new and fascinating stranger who gazed back at her from the mirror. She experienced a strange sensation in the pit of her stomach. She held out her hands and looked at her carefully filed and polished fingernails. She glanced at her reflection again, then walked to the bathroom where she took nail polish remover from her cosmetic bag and quickly wiped the polish off. Then, with determination, she picked up her nail clippers and ruthlessly clipped the nails back to her fingertips in a square, blunt fashion.

D1602797

*For Mae
and Denise,
our sisters*

BIOGRAPHICAL STATEMENT

Shelley Smith, the pseudonym of two writers living in the Boston area, published HORIZON OF THE HEART in 1986. THE PEARLS is their second collaborative work.

THE PEARLS

by Shelley Smith

The Naiad Press, Inc.
1987

Printed in the United States of America
First Edition

Cover design by The Women's Graphic Center
Typesetting by Sandi Stancil
Editor: Katherine V. Forrest

ISBN 0-930044-93-2

I

Harriet Pearl watched the last of her familiar reflection fade from sight, relieved that this stage of the transformation was complete. It had been a long afternoon at Mel's Salon, but as the hours passed she had begun to accept that the assignment, no matter how difficult, would not be impossible.

"Like what you see?" Mel asked cheerfully. "Or should I say *who* you see?"

"I'm not sure," Harriet answered slowly, thinking that no one had said she had to like this. "But you've done a good job."

"Only good?" He twirled the chair around so that she faced him. "Aren't you the hard one to please? It's superb!

Remember what you looked like when you walked in here?"

"Of course," Harriet said, lamenting her thick blonde curls now cut and clipped into a style befitting a conservative Midwesterner. She ran her fingertips across thick, bristly eyebrows. She touched her cheek and quickly withdrew her hand. The base makeup made her skin feel rough and look suspiciously grey. "People will think I have five o'clock shadow," she said mournfully, her voice a rumble of low-pitched tones.

"Wonderful," he cried. "Success! Success! And with that voice of yours, one would think Tallulah Bankhead herself had stepped back into the room." He crossed his arms and rapidly tapped his thumb against the sleeve of a fuschia smock. "All I ask of you, my handsome young man, is two tickets to opening night of the play. Somewhere in the first ten rows—on the aisle, if possible."

"Sure," Harriet said, trying to generate enthusiasm. After all, she thought, Mel had succeeded.

For show business cosmetology and makeup, Mel was the best in New York. He'd been told that Harriet Pearl had been cast as the leading man in an off-Broadway play.

"Harry-Harriet," Mel said with a laugh, "don't look so grim." He twirled the chair again so that Harriet faced her reflection. "With the punk look all the rage, you'll be right in style . . . when you're not in drag, that is. Just brush your hair up and forward instead of straight back."

Harriet had a sudden glimpse of herself as others might see her. She smiled at the reflection. I do make a pretty good looking guy, she thought, at least from the neck up.

"Even you like what you see, don't you?" Mel asked. "What'd I tell you? Impossible to resist! Next I want you to see my assistant, she'll explain some of the procedures so you don't have to come running in here every time you think your beard is disappearing. It'll be a few minutes, she's with another client."

"I'm not in any hurry," Harriet replied. "I need to absorb this new look gradually . . . very gradually."

"You're going to love it, hon," he said, "just give yourself a day or two."

In the mirror, she followed Mel's reflection to the black laminated desk at the center of the large salon. As he spoke with the receptionist, Harriet took another look at herself.

"Bunny is not going to believe this," she said aloud. How would she ever summon the courage to face her partner?

She reached into her purse for cigarettes and a lighter and was momentarily disconcerted as she brought a manicured hand to her mouth, the frosted melon polish a startling contrast to the unfamiliar face that stared back from the mirror. As she looked at her hands, she thought of how long it had taken the nails to grow and how carefully she'd applied the polish just that morning. Now the nails would have to be clipped, the polish removed. Then what? What else would she have to do? Was there even a chance that this scheme of Stillwell's would work?

And what was behind it all? She knew Stillwell wasn't happy with women doing anything more than routine office work. He'd made no secret of his disappointment when she was first assigned to him as junior agent. And when Bunny Silver had signed on eight years ago, he'd become openly hostile to the notion of women working for the Agency. He only took pleasure in the fact that there was no love lost between the women.

Harriet believed that one of his long-range objectives was to force their resignations. So what was going on now? Did he think they could do this job or was he setting them up to justify their dismissal or demotion?

* * * * *

3

Fourteen unfulfilled years as a junior agent had led directly to Harriet's uncertainty about the part she was to play in this latest scheme devised by Victor Stillwell, division chief of the New York branch of Caribbean Sea Watch, their Washington-based agency.

An honor student in college, she'd majored in Criminal Justice believing it would lead to a job with one of the intelligence agencies of the United States government. Her dream had been of a career filled with adventure and travel, and though her friends had advised against it, she'd applied to the top agency, the CIA. The preliminary interview was a long one which she'd passed with flying colors. But their response stated that as favorably impressed as the Agency was, there were no openings at present. Because of potential budget cutbacks, it seemed unlikely that any hiring would be done in the near future.

She'd thought of applying to the F.B.I. but their agents were required to have three years of full-time work experience as well as a college degree. Back then, that seemed an eternity to Harriet, and finding a job that she felt would provide relevant work experience wasn't easy. After a number of disappointing interviews, she took an interim position as a security guard for a lumberyard, using the lonely hours to read and to plan her future. In time, however, her future included Roger Wills, an ambitious law student from the Midwest.

Their marriage was brief. If moving to Nebraska had taught her nothing else, it was that her dreams were not to be surrendered or abandoned. A year later, she was overjoyed when she was contacted by Caribbean Sea Watch, a small agency funded by the CIA. With a staff of nearly fifty, the function of CSW was to gather and sift information pertaining to the growing diplomatic corps in South America and to investigate any suspected or potential irregularities.

She'd presented the news of the job offer to Roger, knowing that this was not a subject for debate. She'd already decided to accept.

Roger had warned her that it wouldn't work; they could not maintain a cross-country relationship. She soon learned that he was right but she wouldn't resign. Some months later, on one of their occasional visits, he told her that he had met someone, a woman from his hometown, that they had been seeing each other, that he wanted a divorce. She wasn't surprised.

To this day she remembered her high excitement at the move east. The Agency job was a start, and she was determined to prove her abilities, to make senior agent within three years. But over fourteen years the dreams of excitement had faded, replaced by dull assignments and endless bureaucratic paper work passed on by the division chief, Victor Stillwell.

Until now.

This assignment has got to be a plum for the Agency, she mused. Intelligence had come up from Washington that Alan Turner, the American Consul to Venezuela, was suspected of covert involvement with General Hosada and his wife Maria, rulers of the peaceful Caribbean nation of Los Pagos. Turner had met the Hosadas last year while on holiday. He had returned to the Presidential Palace several times in the past months, had requested an indefinite leave of absence from his post, and had now taken up residence on the island nation twenty miles southeast of Trinidad.

Hosada, who had ruled Los Pagos since a revolution thirty years ago, maintained a peaceful life for the island's half million inhabitants. Why, then, was intrigue developing now?

Turner, a respected careerist, had only his recent divorce to blemish a record which spanned decades. Reports were that he had taken the General's wife as his mistress—that she and the General were wooing Turner for substantial sums of money. The Agency needed to know the source of Turner's money and for what purpose it would be used.

If Turner's wife hadn't left him, Stillwell had intoned in the briefing, he might have been able to make substantial contributions to the General's treasury—but surely not on a Consul's salary. Turner had married money and money had walked away from him. Turner had even asked his former brothers-in-law for large personal loans and been rebuffed.

"Desperate, wouldn't you say?" Stillwell asked. "Should be easy to find out what he's up to and it shouldn't take much time."

Stillwell leafed through the pages of the report which had been developed out of information from an informer on the island who was one of Maria Hosada's many ex-lovers. Spurned by Maria when Alan Turner caught her attention, he had made the trip personally to Caracas to report his story to one of Turner's staff who conveyed the details to Washington. The informer was described as a "pretty boy"—the only type Maria Hosada ever found attractive. Earlier reports confirmed that over the years she'd acquired a "kennel of these toy poodles."

Stillwell laughed at the phrase as he continued reading from the lengthy document. That she'd chosen Turner as the informant's replacement when she and the General decided the Consul might be a source of financial funds was perhaps speculation—but it was informed speculation.

"If this is really the situation," Stillwell said, "all we need to do is send down another Romeo—but a Romeo who's loaded with big bucks. Someone who's real competition, someone to take this lady's mind off Tuner. That way, the competition will force his hand—and whatever he's got in mind."

Harriet shrugged and exchanged a puzzled glance with Bunny, thinking there was nothing in this for them. Their usual function at CSW was to analyze reports submitted by senior field agents. These were due at the end of each month and were of such a routine nature that the data was generally evaluated in a few days. The rest of the time, Harriet and Bunny performed office duties deemed appropriate by Stillwell, though they had been assigned to the Langmaid stakeout last summer. That had taken them only as far as Brooklyn Heights, she remembered ruefully. Postage stamps were all they'd seen of South America since signing on with CSW. Harriet turned her attention back to Stillwell.

"We've got two important pieces of information," he said. "First, Turner is interested enough in whatever the Hosadas are dangling under his nose to have asked his former wife's family for cash. Second, this Maria Hosada harbors a liking for these delicate . . . genteel men."

His eyes glistened with excitement as he spoke. "We're going to set up a double whammy that'll fix Turner for good—and we're going to get things moving right here. He's in town now, Turner is, hosting one big society bash after another, trying to sniff out would-be investors. We'll start the ball rolling by getting the Consul to invite the prettiest boy we can find down to this lovely island. He's going to be one *rich* pretty boy to boot."

Stillwell sneered, "Notice, I didn't say *fag*. The lady likes real men, they just have to dress like fags, act like fags." He leaned back in his chair and took a cigarette out of his shirt pocket. "We don't have anybody like that in this office or *any* of the Intelligence agencies of the U.S. of A. No fags, goddamnit, and no switch hitters that look like fags either." He reached into the pocket for his lighter, a thin silver cylinder engraved with his initials. A bright flame flickered under his nose as Stillwell inhaled; then he hunched his shoulders and leaned across the table to capture the attention of his staff. "I've figured a way around the lady's weird tastes." He licked his thin lips, spit out a shred of tobacco and smiled. "Now here's the plan," he said in a hushed voice.

"We've got a Washington contact in place already, Warren Bragg. This operation is top secret, though. The details go no further than this office for now. Bragg isn't going to know much, but he doesn't have to. He'll be our social secretary—so to speak—make all the introductions.

"Our own man will be bait for Turner *and* Maria Hosada—rich enough to interest the Consul, pretty enough to cast a spell over the Señora. So, while he works his way into her . . . confidence, he'll be enticement for Turner at the same time."

"Who's playing Romeo?" Bunny asked. "Going to get a wig for Driscoll? Better give him some acting lessons while you're at it." She smiled broadly, then laughed, her loud, throaty tones filling the air.

"If I could send Driscoll or any of the *men,* I would," he said, "but this calls for something subtle." He paused for effect and then continued, "We'll give this Maria a pretty boy, all right, and just to prove our pretty boy isn't a fag, we'll send him down with his little woman." Then he smiled broadly as he looked across the table. "Silver. Pearl. You're it. You're going to Los Pagos as man and wife."

Mr. Mel's assistant stepped into the booth. "Well, aren't you the handsome gent? An actress, are you? Pleased to meet you, I'm Lorraine."

Before Harriet had a chance to answer the wiry, bespectacled young woman, Lorraine pulled up a stool, sat down next to her and proceeded to deliver a thirty minute lecture on makeup and cosmetology that had Harriet's head spinning. Then Lorraine told Harriet to stand.

"Come on, babe, turn around. Face me. What size bra do you wear?"

"What?" Harriet resented the question. "Why?"

"This is no time to be bashful. Thirty-six A? I'm right, aren't I? I tell you girl, you're lucky. All you'll have to do is tape your tits down and wear a heavy T-shirt. If that. Come on."

Harriet followed Lorraine into a small lounge where Mel sat in front of a color TV. He looked up and smiled. "Mel's makeup covers the better parts of the best-known stars," he proclaimed, and pointed to the set. "I'm the makeup consultant for this show, you know." Then he took a careful look at Harriet. "Put you in a three-piece suit right now and I'd wager you could fool most anyone. From the waist up, I could go for you myself."

For only a second, Harriet was confused by his comment.

"Don't take it to heart, I'm just kidding." He noticed the tube of ointment in Harriet's hand. "Don't forget to use that after you take off your makeup. It's the only thing I know of that's guaranteed to keep your face from breaking out."

Then Harriet caught a glimpse of herself in the full-length mirror behind the TV. She wore a pleated paisley skirt, white long-sleeved blouse with ruffled collar and cuffs, and sling-back heels. She carried a large tan purse.

"I can't go out on the streets looking like this," she said. "My face doesn't match my outfit."

Mel laughed. "You are *so* right, Harry-Harriet. But this is *New York* not Salt Lake City. Grab a cab, get where you're going, make yourself a stiff drink, and *re-lax*!"

Mel was right. The cab driver didn't give Harriet a second look but when she walked into the lobby of the Barbizon Hotel it was a different story. The small lobby was crowded with tourists. An insistent and impatient tour guide was attempting to register his bus load of weary travelers, and as Harriet made her way through the men and women, she felt as if she were walking a gauntlet of curious stares. She moved quickly to the elevator hoping she'd be able to ride up to her room alone, but several hotel guests joined her in the small car. A chubby teenaged boy snickered as he looked at Harriet, while the mother, who placed a protective hand on her son's shoulder, glared her disapproval. It was a slow ride to the twelfth floor.

She walked quickly to the room she was sharing with her partner, Bunny Silver, and tapped quietly on the cream-colored door. A bellboy walked by and winked. She glared at him until he turned the corner, then tapped again. There was still no answer. She began to pound on the door, her hand clutched in a tight fist.

"I'm coming as fast as I can, hold your horses," Bunny called.

Bunny opened the door and Harriet whisked by her and turned around, an angry expression on her face.

"Why didn't you just use your key?" Bunny asked sweetly.

"I forgot it," Harriet grumbled. "But in the future," she said sharply, "I'd like an immediate response. We're partners in this assignment, my life could depend on you." She threw herself into a chair and kicked off her heels.

Bunny was smiling. "My, how strong and assertive you've already become," she said teasingly. "Just goes to show you what a little makeup can do for a girl."

Harriet wasn't amused.

Bunny took a careful look. What a beautiful looking

guy, she thought. How can that be? As a woman, she's average at best. . . . As a man, she's a knockout. If what Stillwell says about the General's wife is true, she's going to flip over Harriet.

"You look great," Bunny exclaimed. "You'll break hearts wherever you go, but I don't think you should wear skirts anymore. Even in the privacy of our own home. We've got to go shopping."

"I'm not going anywhere looking like this," Harriet said. "Can't you go out and buy me some jeans and a shirt?"

"Sure, what size?"

"Twelve," Harriet answered.

"I'm going to the men's department," Bunny said, amused by Harriet's predicament. "Let's see, about a size fifteen shirt, twenty-eight long pants, nine narrow shoes, shorts and undershirts size small—"

"You think I'm wearing men's shorts?" Harriet interrupted, her voice rising.

"Don't worry, I'll pick out pastel shades. The new jockey shorts are very pretty," she joked.

After Bunny left, Harriet walked to the mirror and stared at herself. With the initial shock worn off, she looked quizzically at this new and fascinating stranger who gazed back at her from the mirror. She experienced a strange sensation in the pit of her stomach. She held out her hands and looked at her carefully filed and polished fingernails. She glanced at her reflection again, then walked to the bathroom where she took nail polish remover from her cosmetic bag and quickly wiped the polish off. Then, with determination, she picked up her nail clippers and ruthlessly clipped the nails back to her fingertips in a square, blunt fashion.

She unbuttoned her blouse, stepped out of her skirt

11

and was about to turn on the shower when she remembered her makeup. Don't want that to run, she told herself, and put on her flowered robe to wait for Bunny's return. When she heard the key in the door two hours later, she hurried over and unhooked the chain-lock.

"What'd you buy?" Harriet asked excitedly.

"Whatever it is sure isn't going to go with the robe," Bunny said. "Get rid of it. We'll pick you up a man's terry cloth number later. Here you go," she said, tossing four paper bags in Harriet's direction. She watched while Harriet took out a pair of grey linen trousers, a black silk sport shirt, black loafers, and six pairs of bright red jockey shorts.

"Sorry they're all the same color," Bunny said. "I forgot the undershirts. We'll pick some up later."

"Do I really have to wear these?" Harriet asked, holding up a pair of the shorts.

"Sure do. You never know when you'll be stripped to your skivvies."

"You think this plan is going to work, don't you?"

"Of course. How do you like the slacks? I thought jeans were too casual. We're traveling first class now."

"They're all right, but black's not my color," she said, holding up a long-sleeved silk shirt.

"You'll look great in it. Come on, get dressed and we'll go out for a fast bite. You need to get a feel for how people will react to you as a man."

Harriet took the clothes into the bathroom, stepped out of her robe, rolled it into a ball, dropped it into the waste basket. She took the shorts out of their plastic wrapper and stepped into them. Not bad, she thought. I look better in these than I do in my bikini. She slipped the shirt on next and as she was about to button the cuffs, she looked at herself in the mirror, smiled, and rolled the sleeves back at a jaunty angle. She buttoned the shirt, liking the shirttails which cut across her lean body in a curve that scooped out her thighs, completely covering the red shorts. She stepped into the slacks and zippered the fly. Not bad for a quick shopping spree, she thought. She combed back her blonde hair, turned, and opened the door.

"What do you think?" she asked.

"I'll be damned," Bunny said in amazement.

They both laughed.

"So where shall we eat?" Harriet asked, trying to sound casual.

"Let's try the hotel café. We'll grab a bite and plan a real shopping binge for tomorrow."

Harriet reached for her purse, held it between two fingers, dropped it. "Guess I can't take this with me."

Bunny handed her a slim leather billfold. "Here you go, Harriet—or should I say *Harry?* Credit cards, cash, travelers' checks—all in the package from headquarters."

Harriet took the billfold and turned it over in her hand, then slipped it into her back pocket.

Harriet felt surprisingly at ease as she followed Bunny from the elevator and through the lobby to the café. The room was attractive, with mirrors running along the side and back walls which reflected the late afternoon sunlight streaming in from windows facing the street. They chose a small table near the ornately carved oak bar.

As Bunny spread the last of the Brie on a crust of French bread she asked, "Shall we order more herring, or is it time to move on to dessert?"

"I'm content with the wine," Harriet replied, "you have whatever you like."

"All right," she said brightly. "I'm having the peach

13

melba. Rich, sweet and gooey. Aren't you tempted?"

"No," Harriet said emphatically. "I'm not one for desserts in the middle of the day."

"How *interesting*, Harry. Just *think* of all that we're going to know about each other by the time we finish this assignment."

A short time later, as Bunny licked the last of the raspberry syrup from the spoon, she said, "I think your disguise is working. Did you notice how attractive our waitress found you?"

Harriet ignored Bunny's question and concentrated on her wine. She knew she'd blushed at the waitress's smile. It was strange having a woman respond to her like this. She looked over at Bunny who was smirking.

"What are you grinning at?" Harriet asked defensively. "She was probably just looking for a big tip."

In a surprisingly subtle move, Bunny gestured to the next table where a tall, voluptuous woman was just being seated. "That woman can't take her eyes off you. We'll have to get you a wedding band, Harry," Bunny said laughingly. "There's got to be some way to keep these women away from you."

"What?" Harriet asked, feeling as stunned by the comment as she was by the woman's gaze.

"Oh, go ahead and flirt with her," Bunny said. "It'll be good practice for you. I'm going to the john."

"Not without me you don't," Harriet said.

"Honey, do I have to remind you that we use separate facilities now?"

Bunny saw the look of frustration on her face. "Harriet, can't you wait till we get upstairs?"

"Of course, that's not it. I just feel all thumbs. I don't know what to do with myself."

"Just sit here and finish your coffee while I go powder my nose. Then we'll get you that wedding band. I always said that if I ever married, my husband would wear a ring."

"Whatever makes you happy, dear," Harriet said in a tone of resignation.

"Good. Now lower your voice a shade more . . . and be here when I get back."

"Where else can I go like this?" Harriet folded her napkin and placed it beside the empty plate.

In their hotel room once more, they spent the rest of the evening going over their cover stories. Tomorrow they would begin quizzing each other until the covers were down pat, every detail committed to memory. By 11:00, Harriet was exhausted.

"Too much for one day, eh?" Bunny asked.

"Maybe. I'm just going to turn in," she said, anxious to remove the heavy makeup.

In the bathroom she looked at herself in the mirror. Now that the initial novelty had worn off, she felt the burden of her disguise. What if she made a mistake? What if she were found out? After removing her makeup, she wearily applied the skin ointment Mel had given her.

"What's wrong?" Bunny asked as Harriet hung her slacks and shirt in the closet. "You look so glum."

"I feel glum. In every way, I'm going to have to pay a higher price than you for this assignment."

"What do you mean?" Bunny was buffing her nails.

"I'll be wearing T-shirts and Fruit-of-the-Loom jockey shorts to bed. I'll probably end up with some kind of skin disease from this makeup and—"

"Stop whining," Bunny said with a shrug. "You know

you make a better looking guy than I do. Besides, you're taller. And look at the new social scene it opens up for you."

Harriet closed the closet door and walked to her bed. It wasn't worth discussing her feelings with Bunny. All she wanted was a good night's sleep.

"You don't regret taking this assignment, do you?" Bunny asked in a more serious tone.

Harriet glanced toward the ceiling. Earlier, they'd checked the hotel room and weren't surprised when they found a CSW bug in the smoke detector. They'd figured that Stillwell would plant one somewhere.

"It's still out," Bunny said, acknowledging her glance. "We'll have to connect the bug back up before we go to sleep."

"Right. No, I don't regret the assignment," Harriet said thoughtfully, "but I don't trust Victor. Not for a minute. This is one hell of a crazy idea. Do you think this is part of a plan to get us out of CSW? Is he setting us up?"

"Maybe. But I don't intend to lose sleep over it and neither should you. Between the two of us we've logged a lot of hours and we're still in the same place we were when we started out. Finally we have the chance to be more than gofers. I think we should make the most of it."

"True," Harriet reponded. "I guess we can protect each other."

"Of course. I'm sure Victor has already taken bets that we won't last twenty-four hours together."

Harriet laughed. "That's probably the setup right there. He thinks we can't do it."

"He's in for a big surprise, isn't he?" Bunny commented.

Harriet smiled her agreement.

"Now you look better," Bunny said with enthusiasm. "Let's get up early and spend the day shopping. I intend to

16

make full use of the charge cards to all those fancy stores. On our salaries, I haven't dared to walk into most of them."

Exhausted from the day, Harriet slept soundly. Bunny found herself waking at odd moments in the night, aware of Harriet's presence in the room.

That morning it took Harriet longer than either woman expected to get ready. She had trouble with her makeup and her hair hadn't settled into its new cut. Eventually, between the efforts of the two of them, Harriet emerged as Harry and they enjoyed a leisurely stroll to a French café on Madison Avenue where they had breakfast.

"Don't get discouraged, Harry," Bunny said, buttering a warm croissant. "By the end of the week you'll be able to put that makeup on in the dark, but that perfume has *got* to go. You should be wearing after-shave lotion. I'll pick some up for you, I like choosing scents for my fellas."

"I learned a long time ago not to buy a guy anything special, it's usually not appreciated. What about your fiancé," Harriet asked with curiosity, "does he really appreciate the nice things you try to do for him?"

"I'm not talking about Bert, I'm talking about my . . . casual dates."

"You must buy it by the case," Harriet said coolly.

"Cut it out right now," Bunny said sharply. "We can't afford to go back to clawing one another. There's no more Harriet. No more Bunny Silver. Just Mr. and Mrs. Pearl. Agreed?"

Harriet nodded in assent as Bunny smiled sweetly.

"Now Harry," she continued, emphasizing the name, "do you think we'll be going to that island soon? We'd better pick out a few tropical suits for you."

Harriet was surprised at how much fun their shopping trip was. She'd always thought that most men wore two uniforms: one for play and one for work. Only the cut of suit, the color of shirt, the pattern of tie announced both status and style. It seemed predictable—but dull.

Most gay men, though, dressed with imagination and flair, and, Harriet vowed, that was the way she would dress. Give them something to remember down in Los Pagos.

At Madison Avenue and 72nd Street, they admired the exterior of the Rhinelander mansion, one of the recent acquisitions of the Ralph Lauren empire. The five story neoclassical building was constructed of intricately carved dark cream limestone. A blue awning hung over the gleaming brass-railed steps of the main entrance. Imaginatively designed display windows caught their attention as they crossed the street. It all looked very inviting.

"Do you think Stillwell's budget can cover the Polo store?" Harriet asked.

"Let's put it to the test," Bunny said, with a mischievous twinkle in her eye.

They walked through the double-glass doors of the main entrance toward a beige carpeted staircase. On the dark green felt-covered walls of the stairwell hung a collection of 19th century prints which they stopped to admire.

"Have the feeling you're in a museum? Are you sure this is the place we should shop?" Harriet asked.

Bunny reached for Harriet's hand. "Oh, let's give it a try," she said, leading Harriet up the stairs. "After all, how much can a few shirts cost?"

They were the only customers in the Polo room that Tuesday morning and consequently enjoyed the full attention of the friendly salesman.

Bunny and Harriet's spirits were high and Claude picked up their mood. He began joking with them, then as his humorous remarks turned to camp, the banter took on a flavor that was unmistakably gay. As he selected a white linen blazer from the collection, he winked at Harriet.

My God, Harriet thought, what *is* going on? Women in the Barbizon Café . . . Nice, middle-aged salesmen . . . Who *is* this Harry Pearl?

"Harry," Bunny called over, "come try on one of these jackets with padded shoulders."

"The natural look is much better for him," Claude said. "He's not the shoulder-pads type."

"Is that so? I think I know what looks best on my husband, if you don't mind."

"Of course, Madame, I only meant with regard to current styles—"

"We do *not* need advice on current styles," Bunny responded haughtily, realizing that a large part of her job would be running interference for Harriet.

"Bunny, why don't you wait here while I try on a few suits," Harriet said. "If I think they're right, I'll come out for your approval."

"Isn't that the way we've always chosen your wardrobe? But you," she said, looking at Claude, "are staying with me."

"Naturally, Madame," Claude replied, as he directed his attention to a loose button on a classic navy blazer.

A short time later, Harriet's new wardrobe had been selected: slacks, sports jackets, and suits. They would shop for shirts and ties on the first floor. So far they had spent a small fortune.

"Mr. Pearl," Claude said sweetly, "could you step this way for your packages?"

As they stood at the wrapping desk, he turned to Harriet and said, "Your appointment with Alterations is Friday at eleven. Care to have lunch when you're finished?"

19

"No," Harriet said uncomfortably, "I'm with her. All the way."

"My mistake, Mr. Pearl. If you change your mind, I could be free for an hour or so any day next week."

Harriet took the card Claude handed her and slipped it into her pants pocket just as Bunny walked up behind them.

"Are we ready, darling?" Bunny asked.

"He's all yours," Claude said. "See you Friday . . . if not before."

"What did he mean by that?" Bunny inquired as they walked to the elevator.

"Who knows, *darling*?" Harriet said, emphasizing the endearment. "What do you think?" She displayed Claude's business card; he'd written his home phone number under his name.

"Wonderful," Bunny said. "You, *Harry,* are supposed to be delicate—not gay. Stop flirting with guys."

"This isn't as easy as it looks. I thought he was cute. Imagine if you had to stop flirting with guys? And how do you know he was gay?"

Bunny ignored the question. "Harry," she said, "this is not going to be easy. First, we have to create the right impression for Alan Turner. We have to appear wealthy . . . securely married . . . in love even. We have to work it so that he invites us to that island. But then, once down there, you have to catch the attention of the General's wife. We've been *told* about the men she goes for. M-E-N. Get it?"

"It's going to take some time to believe I'm a man, to believe I'm *Harry* Pearl."

"You don't have time," Bunny said impatiently. "Look, enjoy this, don't be a drudge. I've already decided you're my husband and I'm going to relish every moment of it.

20

I've never been married, there's a good chance Bert and I will never take the plunge, so now's my chance to play let's pretend. How many women have the opportunity you do—how many women can switch roles? Haven't you ever wondered what it's like to be a man? Now's your chance to find out. Enjoy some of these macho privileges. See how people respond to you as Harry Pearl. When you go back to being Harriet, you're bound to have learned a few things."

Harriet smiled at Bunny's intensity. She was seeing a different side of her partner, a practical yet very determined side. Bunny was right—to succeed at their assignment, she *had* to become Harry Pearl. Hey, she thought, if she can make the most of it, so can I.

She grabbed Bunny's hand as they walked down the street and playfully squeezed her fingers. Then, as Bunny broadly smiled at Harriet, their palms clasped, fingers entwined. Bunny's hand felt tiny to Harriet, soft and smooth. Harriet experienced a giddy sensation at the realization of holding another woman's hand, yet the feeling also was very pleasant. She felt surprisingly secure as she walked hand in hand with Bunny.

"I've got my new wardrobe, Bunny, let's get started on yours," Harriet said.

They strolled down Madison Avenue, passing salons and boutiques neither woman had visited before: Rive Gauche, Missoni, Gianni Versace, Giorgio Armani.

"I can't even pronounce the names of these places," Harriet joked. "Can you imagine the price tags?"

Bunny giggled. "We've got to dress the part, don't we?"

"Absolutely," Harriet replied with conviction, holding up her bag from Ralph Lauren's Polo store.

At the intersection, they stopped for the red light, surrounded by other shoppers enjoying the crisp autumn

21

afternoon. In the next block they paused in front of a narrow, white granite building. "La Boutique de Simone—my favorite shop, Harry. In all of New York. I've never been able to do more than window-shop. Do we dare go in?"

"Of course, my dear," Harriet said, ceremoniously opening the door and stepping back for Bunny to pass.

"Talk about let's pretend," Bunny squealed. "No matter what else happens on this whacky assignment, this afternoon's going to make it all worthwhile."

Tempted to browse through the collection with Bunny, Harriet thought it best to accept the plush velvet chair offered to her by one of the saleswomen. Now it was Harriet's turn to agree or disagree on Bunny's choices. She smiled at the expression on Bunny's face as she approved several dresses.

Harriet leaned back in her chair and relaxed as she was offered a glass of champagne. She drank it quickly and decided that she liked this new, elegant dimension to shopping. Her glass was always full and after the third refill, as the chic saleswoman leaned to pour just a touch more of the sparkling champagne, she touched Harriet's shoulder, her fingers lingering ever so gently along the back of Harriet's neck.

"I'd better not have any more," Harriet said, "my wife will take advantage of me and buy out the store!"

"Oh, we'd never let her do that," she was told with a smile.

"Why not?"

The saleswoman only laughed as she returned the champagne to its silver ice bucket.

Just then Bunny appeared before Harriet in a low-cut burgundy silk dress. "How do you like it?" she asked.

Harriet smiled in approval, taking in the fullness of Bunny's figure now sculpted into a classic hourglass by the

22

lines of the dress. As Bunny stepped across the thick carpet her movements were exaggerated, a studied mimicry of stereotyped notions of femininity. With a sultry sway, her deep-set grey eyes sparkling, she walked back and forth in front of Harriet who now viewed her from the double perspective of being Bunny's partner as well as Bunny's husband.

Harriet admired her soft features, generous mouth, rich olive skin. Bunny's thick brown hair was styled in a blunt cut that just touched the line of her jaw. Although she was small-boned and only a few inches over five feet tall, her figure was voluptuous—full breasts, a tiny waist, gently curving hips and long shapely legs. Harriet took all of her in with a critical eye as she scanned the length of Bunny's body.

Harriet was offered more champagne and Bunny asked coyly, "Do you like this color on me, sweetheart?"

When Harriet didn't reply, Bunny took in the scene. She noticed the woman attending Harriet and felt annoyed.

"Harry," she said sharply, "look at me." Then she addressed the saleswoman. "How do you like it?"

"Stunning, Madame," the woman replied.

"Thank you. Is it available in another color? I want something dressy, but warmer. A rose shade, perhaps, or a delicate pink. My husband's found burgundy too severe."

The saleswoman smiled at Bunny. "I think we have just what you're looking for." She turned and walked to the rear of the salon.

"Okay, Harry," Bunny said with deliberation, "I meant it when I said I wanted some of your attention. Stop letting these women wrap you around their little fingers!"

"Claude wasn't a woman," Harriet said, crossing her legs as she set the champagne glass on the small marble table at her side.

23

"Wonderful," Bunny said sarcastically. "Now what about this dress? Like it on me?"

"Very much. But as the wife of Harry Pearl, I think you need to dress conservatively. Just like the birdies in the trees, Bunny, I wear the fancy plumage. Besides, you don't want to compete with Maria."

"I should have known this would all go to your head in a matter of hours," Bunny sourly replied. "Lay off the champagne."

She knew Harriet was right, though, and in a tone of resignation added, "All right, I'll pick a basic black, a few pastels for daytime wear and a culotte skirt. Conservative enough?"

"Sure. And one dress to suit your heart's desire. Even if you don't wear it on this assignment, Victor said we get to keep our clothes, remember?"

"Looks as if yours are beginning to grow on you," Bunny said sharply as she turned in the direction of the dressingroom.

Minutes later Bunny walked toward Harriet, three dress boxes stacked in a large glossy shopping bag. Harriet stood and took the bag from her.

"All ready?" Harriet asked brightly.

"This is just a start. We have to plan for all the activities that will be part of life on Los Pagos."

"Such as?"

"The beach, for one thing—"

"Oh no," Harriet broke in, "we can only push our luck so far."

"Don't be an ass, Pearl. We'll pick up a few cabana suits for you. Just remember to keep the tops buttoned."

"What else?"

"We'll make a list," Bunny said.

"My head's pounding," Harriet replied, "it's the champagne. Let's go have some lunch."

Harriet ordered a Jack Daniels on the rocks to settle her stomach and ease her headache, then leaned back in her chair and asked Bunny for a cigarillo.

"Why?" Bunny asked. "You despise them. How many times have you left the office when I've just wanted to relax and have a quiet smoke?"

"I know what I'm doing, Bunny. From now on, you smoke regulation filter cigarettes, I smoke cigarillos . . . until I get hold of some first-class cigars."

"Great," Bunny said in disgust. "And what are you going to order for lunch? Your usual green salad?"

"Does Harry Pearl strike you as the kind of man to eat *salads*? I'll have the grilled lamb kidneys. Rare."

As the waiter approached their table with the bourbon, Harriet smiled and looked over at Bunny. "Having your usual glass of white wine, dear?"

II

Bunny and Harriet used the remainder of their time before meeting with Victor to master their cover stories, complete their purchases, and resolve any personal differences which might prevent the two of them from successfully fulfilling the assignment.

Harriet was becoming a distant relative for Harry while at the same time, Harry was becoming Harriet's ideal man. When she looked at herself in the mirror each morning, she was no longer sure of whom she was seeing. She felt a gradual merging of two people.

As the following week passed, she and Bunny became increasingly confident of their stories and rarely fell out of place in playing their roles as the Pearls. An easy friendliness developed which would have surprised them only a few weeks ago. Come evening, rather than picking up the newspaper or turning on the TV, they spent their hours in casual conversation.

Their frequent subject was Victor Stillwell. Over the years Bunny had been intimate with a variety of her fellow agents and now she gladly shared pillow talk with Harriet about Victor.

Harriet, who never mixed business with pleasure, was fascinated by the bits and pieces of Agency gossip which Bunny now passed her way. She'd long questioned Victor's mental stability and often wondered how he managed to hold onto his position as Assistant Regional Director of the Agency.

Bunny, curled up on the plush mauve sofa, her purple robe tied snugly around her waist, said, "What you probably don't know about the old man is, he was a terrific field agent. He'd take any assignment no matter how dangerous—or dirty, either. One of the fellows told me the attitude up high was, no matter how twisted or obsessive Stillwell might seem, he was essential to the Agency. He had only one partner, you know. *Think* about that, Harriet. Somehow he was able to convince headquarters he operated best on his own. After the story I heard from Eddie Burke, I don't know who would *want* to pair up with him."

The expression in Bunny's grey eyes was angry as she arched her eyebrows and crossed her arms. "Eddie gave me all the charming details before he and Donovan were sent down to Nicaragua last year. It goes back years ago to when the boys were in Chile. Eddie Burke, Stillwell and his partner Arch Newton, they were all in the field.

"Newton and Stillwell had completed a major phase of one of the missions that was sure to be successful. A hell of a lot of them *weren't,* if you remember." She continued in a grim voice, the expression in her eyes cool and distant,

27

"Stillwell and Newton were on the run for the jeep they'd hidden in the valley not too far from the post they'd just destroyed. They were being trailed by armed rebels and just as they reached the entrance to the valley, Newton was shot. Stillwell didn't stop, he ran right past him, got to the jeep on his own. He could have tried to hold the rebels off and rescue his partner, but he never even looked back."

"Did he think Newton was dead?" Harriet asked.

"I doubt it. Shouldn't he have checked?"

Bunny stubbed out her cigarette. She spoke softly now. "Burke and Newton were thrown into the same cell for a few hours. Newton had been brutally tortured, Burke knew he'd never make it out. He wanted Burke to know what happened and return the favor to Stillwell sometime.

"Who, Harriet, deserts a partner?" she asked indignantly. "What kind of slime does that? One of the first things Eddie did when he returned to headquarters was talk to his chief. Stillwell's report was airtight, of course. He said the decision he'd made was painful, but the success of the mission came first. There was no time to go back for Newton. And if the situation were reversed, he'd have wanted his partner to do the same."

"What happened to Newton?" Harriet asked quietly.

"I thought you knew," Bunny replied. "They tortured him to death."

She waved her hand in futility. "No one's ever been able to touch Stillwell, but none of us have short memories, do we? I could tell you stories all night long about his threats and his blackmailing tactics, but why deprive us of our beauty sleep? He's a bastard, but he's performed and that's all they care about in Washington. I hear the Agency thinks they have him on a tight leash. He's got to have control—no matter what the price—but they control him and he needs that, too."

28

"And we're putting our lives in his hands?" Harriet exclaimed. "With all you know about him, I'm surprised you've stayed with the Agency as long as you have."

"Where else would I go?" Bunny asked. "It's home for me now—the same way it is for you."

"Why didn't you tell me about this before?"

"How could I? Have we ever really talked to each other before this assignment?"

Harriet, stretched out on a grey Barcalounger, sat upright. "That louse, he's never given us a chance, has he?"

"Does that surprise you?" Bunny asked sarcastically. "From his perspective, what's easier to manipulate than two women?"

"Not two women together," Harriet said with conviction.

Bunny laughed. "What are we?" she asked. "Two women or husband and wife? Don't lose sight of the strings Victor's still pulling."

"I won't, but let's not forget how much Stillwell despises women. Have you ever known him to express an ounce of compassion—even decency—for one? The guy's warped . . . he's rotten . . . " She stood and angrily paced the floor.

Bunny watched her, surprised by the intensity of her emotion. "Harriet, we both know his problems with the fairer—"

"Sex?" Harriet interrupted sharply. "We're a minor problem of his, if you ask me. How did he ever get where he is? Who *ever* thought he could supervise a group of people—men *or* women?"

"I was getting to that," Bunny said in a tone of mild exasperation. "It looks as if this is the night for your history lesson so stop pacing the floor. Sit down and listen. He wasn't taken out of the field and given a desk job until after a car accident that cost him his leg—at least from above the knee. I don't know all the details, but it seems his division chief tried to force him out with a disability pension, and Victor brought certain questionable letters of the chief's to light—"

"That's blackmail," Harriet sputtered. "Why didn't they get rid of him for that?"

Bunny laughed. She was enjoying Harriet's indignation. "How could they?" she asked. "The chief wasn't about to lose his job—which would have happened if these letters had surfaced—so Victor was assigned to *this* office and Samuel Perry. Perry's clean as a whistle, as you know. There's no way Victor could ever get anything on him. Perry keeps his thumb on Victor, Victor keeps us in line and I guess in some crazy way no one's the worse for it. Everyone agrees he's a master at details and he does keep us on our toes, doesn't he?"

"Victor keeps us in line?" Harriet's voice rose in anger. "Is that what you call it, Bunny? We haven't had a chance at anything decent in years—if we ever did—and you say he's good at *details!* We should have blown that jerk away a long time ago."

Harriet walked to the marble mantle and took a cigar, biting off the tip and spitting it out. "So what do you have on him, Silver? Don't hold anything back. I want to know it all."

"Do you now?" Bunny asked coyly.

"Yes," Harriet said. "All the details."

"I wish I could tell you what you want to know but there's only one thing about Victor Stillwell that I'm sure of."

"Go ahead, I'm listening."

"He's clean, Harriet," Bunny said flatly. "I hate to disappoint you but other than being rotten to the core the guy's got no vices—not a one."

"That makes him suspicious right there." Harriet threw herself back into her chair. "What a world," she said in disgust. "He's been allowed to do what most people with normal jobs would be locked up for—"

"Harriet, we don't *have* normal jobs. There's no comparison between—"

"You know what I mean. Whenever you've got a rotten cop or a doctor or an agent—"

"There's no proof that he's rotten."

"What about deserting Arch Newton? What about blackmailing his division chief? What are we? Sitting ducks?"

"No, but I'm not quite sure what we can do. You know my reputation. Just because I've played footsies with an agent or two, Stillwell feels I can't be trusted. Rumor is, I'd distract anyone they hooked me up with . . . as a partner, I mean . . . any man, that is."

"Silver, let out some hot air and bring your head down to size. Who do you think you are? Mata Hari?"

"You don't have to be so cutting," Bunny said, a hurt expression in her eyes.

"I didn't mean to be," Harriet said gently, "I just don't want Stillwell getting the best of us. I'm curious, Bunny— what's your ace?"

"Sam Perry. I'll call him and tip him off that we think something's amiss. I'll ask him to meet us in Stillwell's office next week, *before* the scheduled meeting for the four of us. I suspect Perry only okayed this hare-brained scheme to have the opportunity to finally rid himself of Victor."

"You can't say that."

"I won't. I'll tell him we have a strong feeling Victor is setting us up for a fall and we want him present at these early procedural meetings."

"Kind of like saving two damsels in distress," Harriet said as she crossed her legs and reached for her lighter.

"Not exactly," Bunny laughed. "We want Sam Perry to see how Victor is running this operation. Keep it all professional and above board. Though Perry's probably looking for a way to waltz Victor off to retirement, there's no way he'd put us in a dangerous situation just to deep-six Stillwell. Besides, I really think if Perry finds us believable as the Pearls, it will work."

"I'm impressed," Harriet said, "but if this Maria Hosada is as fast an operator as they say she is, how do I get information from her without becoming—I know this sounds absurd—sexually involved?"

"Because you're a loving and faithful husband," Bunny said quickly. "And Harriet, as a woman you surely know the game of withholding sexual favors until you get what you want."

"Why Mrs. Pearl, I'm starting to see you in a much brighter light than I ever did before."

"Really?"

"Yes I am," Harriet answered with a smile.

As the women enjoyed the warm feeling between them, several moments passed without conversation. Bunny's expression was thoughtful when she looked at Harriet sitting across the room from her. So much was changing between them . . . and so quickly.

"You know why we're getting along so well, Harriet?"

Her blue eyes open wide, Harriet nodded in the affirmative. "We're trying to save our necks. We're pulling together now rather than pushing away. That's why, don't you think?"

"Maybe. Actually, I think your personality is better suited to pants than a skirt."

"That's a lousy comment," Harriet said, her feelings hurt. "I thought we were trying to be friends."

32

"We are. I'm just not saying it right. What I mean is, your serious and ... abrupt manner makes you come off like a tight-assed broad. You have absolutely no sense of humor and ..." Bunny tried to think of a way to erase the frown she saw on Harriet's face. "For example," she continued in a soft voice, "in the past, you've eaten salad for lunch, nothing else, right?"

"How do you know?"

"After all these years don't you think I noticed your little plastic boxes of lettuce in the lunchroom frig? Your major worry seemed to be maintaining your figure, keeping your weight down. Now you're eating like a he-man and I don't see a sign of you adding an ounce."

"What's food have to do with a sense of humor? I'm nervous about all of this," Harriet responded, "so I'm worrying it off. Nothing's different—I've just exchanged worries."

"I think it's more than that. These days together have been the first time we've ever sat around and shot the breeze, know what I mean? Before this, you kept me at such a distance there was no way we could ever exchange more than the bare details of an assignment."

Harriet grinned. "You're right, I've been so intent on getting ahead in the Agency, I've not let my real self get anywhere near the surface. I've maintained what I like to call a neutral profile. You'd probably call it asexual."

"Never said a thing about your sexuality—"

"You don't have to. Don't you think I know what people think about me? Well, I'm not asexual—I've got the divorce papers to prove it. I just didn't want to start sleeping around at the Agency, and I guess I've been so busy with this joke of a career that I haven't taken the time to meet anyone special."

"In all these years?" Bunny asked.

"I'm a master at the deep-six technique," Harriet said flatly.

"What happened to your husband?"

"Roger? He's a lawyer. In Nebraska. He wanted a wife and I wanted a career. It's no more complicated than that."

"Has it been worth it?"

Harriet thought for a moment before answering. "Maybe I haven't succeeded as an agent yet, but at least there's a chance that I will. I know I *never* would have made it as a housewife, no matter *how* many years I'd have stuck it out. Guess I just didn't want to."

Bunny laughed. "What a view of marriage."

"Just marriage to Roger."

"And you actually have that big a stake in your career?"

"Of course. I'd be light-years ahead if I hadn't had someone like Victor peering over my shoulder every minute . . . and a middle-aged Barbie Doll for a partner—"

"What do you mean by that crack?"

"You wanted to talk, didn't you? Since we're having this good old-fashioned lemon squeeze, why don't we just admit that I tried to succeed in my own peculiar way and you, you took the more . . . shall we say, common way? If they still gave awards for helplessness, you'd win ten years out of ten. You *gush* so, Bunny. Why? And you've got this . . . expression, it's like you're still twelve years old when you're talking to one of the guys. Then the way you sleep around. Politically incorrect, to put it mildly."

Harriet continued, "I don't mean to come down so hard on you, but I have to level with you because now I'm starting to see you in a different way. There's a good, solid, practical side to you. You've got common sense, more than I ever figured."

34

Bunny walked across the room and pulled the drapes. "It's getting late."

"I didn't mean to hurt you," Harriet said with concern.

"No? Maybe not. But you're right about me. I thought I could sleep my way to the top. By the time I realized I couldn't, I didn't care anymore and just kept an old habit going."

"How can sex be a habit?" Harriet asked.

"Easily enough," Bunny said quietly. "At least it means I'll probably never marry Bert, though my mother still clings to the hope that I will. Maybe it's my way of saying screw you to Mom. See? Victor isn't the only one in the Agency with problems, is he?"

"No. I'm just glad that in this very strange setting we're becoming close friends."

"Close friends," Bunny repeated, "you're right. If Victor does succeed in doing us in, when we're thrown back into the office pack as permanent gofers, at least we'll know that we can trust each other."

"He's not going to do us in, Bunny, that's the whole point of our talking like this. We're together now."

Victor Stillwell called his secretary into his office.

"Evelyn, haven't those two called in yet? I was sure they'd try to get out of this assignment."

"Pearl and Silver? No, we haven't heard a peep," she said agreeably.

Victor snorted. "They've probably left town." He raised his hand in a motion of dismissal, then handed her a file. "Two of these letters need brief answers, they should be in the afternoon mail."

"I'll get your signature before I leave," she said.

"You sign them," he said, "they're routine correspondence, nothing special."

As Evelyn closed the door behind her, he leaned back, folding his hands behind his head. I've finally got those two where I want them, he thought. Fuck Washington's orders to hire more women, promote within the ranks, follow those goddamn affirmative action guidelines. Fuck Sam Perry too, and the two years he's been on my back to give those broads a chance to make it as senior agents. Neither one of them ever belonged here in the first place. One a stiff-assed old maid, the other a fucking Agency groupie.

Stillwell turned his chair away from the desk, looked out the large picture window facing the East River, and sank into the fantasy which came to him in dreams or, at times such as this, against his will.

The fantasy was played out in different locations: hotel rooms, his own office late at night, his car. Always she came to him, smiling, never speaking, lovingly giving pleasure, exciting and arousing him as no woman ever had. These fantasies were the only way he could master his impulse to approach her, because as much as he desired her, he was equally disgusted by her. He often told himself he should take her—just once, show her what he was all about; yet each time he contemplated this, an image of Bunny came to mind that he could not erase.

She sat before him in a room they shared. The room contained personal effects belonging to them both. She was stretched out on a large, over-stuffed sofa. She wore a robe, nothing else, it was tied loosely about her waist. Her legs were crossed, one foot resting casually over the other. Then she uncrossed her legs and smiled, opening her arms to him. She untied the robe and as he struggled for words to speak to her, she began to laugh. He stepped toward her and she began to laugh all the more. She threw the sash from her robe at him and he grasped at empty air for the silken cord which grew in length separating the two of them until they were at opposite corners of a long, lonely corridor. And still she laughed, the sounds of her voice ringing in his ears.

It was that sound, that image of Bunny laughing which kept him on the other side of his fantasies and, as the stories from the other agents persisted, he was all the more determined that she was not only unworthy of him, beneath him, but she had no place anywhere in the workings of CSW.

Harriet was easier to dismiss. She was merely an overgrown, over-aged Girl Scout and he had no appetite for being her trainer.

He turned back to his desk. They should be getting ready to hand in their resignations about now. Harriet could never pull it off as a man. And Bunny would be snapping at her heels if she *did* try. He had no worries. Even if they showed up, Perry undoubtedly would cancel the assignment.

But what if he approves it? What's my fall-back position? I never made allowances for one. I've gotten sloppy on this desk job. Today's only Wednesday ... We don't meet with Perry until Friday ... I'll screw them up one way or another.

The day of their meeting with Victor they were both awake before dawn.

"D-Day for the Pearls, right Bun?" Harriet asked.

"Do you have to put it that way?" Bunny replied.

"I'm just joking. Come on, *who* doesn't have a sense of humor?"

As Bunny sat up in bed, she looked at Harriet who was warming up for her morning exercises. "Don't you ever take a day off from that routine?" Her voice was edgy with anxiety.

"Never," Harriet answered. "You should join me now and then. It does wonders for your cardiovascular system."

"I'll order coffee. Caffeine gets my cardio-whatever system going just fine. Saves energy, too."

Bunny showered while waiting for room service. She couldn't chase the butterflies that were fluttering in her stomach. Why am I so nervous, she asked herself. I know Harriet and I are believable as a couple. We haven't had a hitch yet. But Victor will be looking for a weak spot, I know that madman. At least he won't be able to say we don't get along as well as we should. We've had a hell of a good time together so far.

"What suit shall I wear today?" Harriet asked as she poured Bunny a cup of fresh coffee.

Bunny looked at Harriet. Her maroon terry cloth robe was tied loosely around her waist, a towel draped casually around her neck. "You're really getting into this aren't you, Pearl?"

"And you're not?" Harriet returned. "So which suit, Bunny?"

"You pick," Bunny said. "And take it easy on the tie, nothing too bright. Victor doesn't like loud ties."

Victor's secretary looked up from the typewriter as a stylishly dressed couple stepped into the room. When she recognized Bunny, she knew the Pearls had arrived. Speechless, she watched them approach her desk as Bunny smoothed her elegantly coiffed hair and affected a dazzling smile.

Harriet's arm was draped around Bunny's waist; she was

smoking a long thin cigar. She inhaled, gestured toward Evelyn and said, "Tell Mr. Stillwell that Mr. and Mrs. Pearl have arrived."

"Of course," she answered, stepping toward Victor's door.

"No, Evelyn, don't go into his office," Harriet ordered, her voice exuding authority. "Buzz him from your desk. We don't want anything to spoil this little surprise, least of all any clues he might receive from you."

"Sure, Harriet," Evelyn said, flustered by these changes in personality, dress, and manner.

"Harriet? There is no Harriet." The voice was even, cool. "I'm Harry Pearl. Got it?"

"Yes sir," she said, feeling uneasy and slightly giddy. As requested, she buzzed Victor on the intercom.

"Mr. and Mrs. Pearl are here to see you, sir," she said.

Victor paused before answering. So they were actually going to try to pull it off. "Give me a minute," he said in response, "then send them in."

Victor sat back in his chair. Something was amiss. He'd given his secretary specific instructions to come into his office in advance of Silver and Pearl. Whatever scheme those two had concocted, it should be rich. They'd be the laughingstock of the Agency before he was through with them.

Victor tensed as the door opened. He looked at the two figures standing in the doorway, took in a deep breath, then exhaled, slowly. He stood, his palms flat on the desk as much for support as effect, as they walked toward him.

Harriet stepped up to the desk, extended a hand. "Hey, fella, good to see you. You remember the missus, don't you?" She reached for Bunny's arm and pulled her up beside her. Sweetly, Bunny extended her hand as well.

Victor ignored the gestures. He sat down and motioned Bunny and Harriet to take the two leather chairs on either side of the desk.

When Samuel Perry walked into the office unannounced, Bunny and Harriet looked at each other and smiled. And Victor knew that he had been taken.

"Am I on time, Ms. Silver?" he asked.

"Right on the dot," Bunny answered.

Victor glared at the women. "Sam, come in," he said, changing his tone and attitude as he welcomed his superior officer. "I didn't think you'd want to take the time to attend this first meeting with the girls ... I mean the Pearls. I know how busy you are and if their cover isn't credible—"

"Let's give them a chance," Sam Perry said. "From the looks of it, I'd say it just might work."

Perry sat down. He decided to enjoy this show. Stillwell wasn't going to get away with anything this time, he thought, taking delight in the pained expression on Victor's face.

Then he looked at Harriet. He couldn't believe the transformation. She looked the part from head to toe. Perry had to hand it to the two of them, they had really pulled it off.

Without giving Victor a chance to control the situation, Bunny and Harriet began talking to each other about their friends in Cleveland. Perry listened as their cover story was presented in the guise of conversation between husband and wife. Harry Pearl reminded his wife of how fortunate they had been to shift the bulk of their monies from the now dying steel industry to foreign investments. With the closing of the first steel mills in Pittsburgh, Harry Pearl had acted quickly and divested the fortune it had taken his father a lifetime to earn. Many of their friends with monies similarly invested had not acted so quickly. For them, the picture was grim. Bunny agreed that it was time to leave Cleveland. Each time Stillwell tried to interrupt, he was ignored. It was as if he wasn't there.

"Ladies," Perry said, "I want to offer my congratulations. You've taken on this assignment with relish and enthusiasm, that's obvious. From what we know of Maria Hosada, Harriet, she is going to find it impossible to resist you. Harry Pearl, you're quite a man."

Harriet winked, sat back in her seat and took Bunny's hand.

"Victor," Perry continued, "this idea of yours is brilliant. I'm impressed, what more can I say?"

"Now just a minute, Sam," Stillwell said, trying to regain his composure. "On second thought, I don't think this *is* such a hot idea. These girls have gone overboard on their role playing. Look at them, sitting there holding hands. I didn't intend to unhinge them, but it looks like that's what's happened. Maybe what they really need is a good long rest and some first-rate counseling."

Perry smiled at the two of them. "Why *are* you holding hands?"

"We were told to be the Pearls twenty-four hours a day," Bunny answered, "and that's what we're doing. We don't let our guard down for a second, do we Harry?"

"Of course not, my dear."

Samuel Perry nodded. "The Pearls are following orders, Stillwell. Anything wrong with that?"

Stillwell didn't answer.

"You're too uptight, Victor," Perry continued. "They won't be into role-playing for long. This assignment's going to be a piece of cake for CSW—thanks to the Pearls."

He turned to Bunny and Harriet. "All you have to do is get Turner to make an offer you can substantiate. When

41

the deal comes down, we'll have him where we want him and you two will be on your way to new assignments as senior agents. On my recommendation," he said, emphasizing his words as he looked at Victor.

Stillwell folded his arms on his chest and said nothing.

"All right," Perry said, "some final details. As you know, we've already got an undercover agent from Washington set in place, Warren Bragg. In a matter of days, he'll introduce you to Turner and you two will take it from there. Victor will keep close contact with you from this point."

Stillwell sat up in his chair. I'll get those two yet, he vowed. Let them have today, I'll be calling the shots tomorrow.

"I want to wish you luck, Pearl. Silver, you, too," Perry said, rising, shaking hands with them. "Call me if you have problems before you leave, but I'd say you have everything under control. Victor, I've got great confidence in this entire operation."

After Perry left, Harriet and Bunny waited for Stillwell's wrath. It was bound to come; Bunny had definitely overstepped boundaries when she had made the special request for Sam Perry to meet them in Stillwell's office. But strangely it didn't come; he wasn't saying anything. Instead, he took out a slim grey folder and gave the Pearls the name and address of The Carlyle, the hotel they were to register at that afternoon. Once settled in their new room, they could expect the call from Bragg within twenty-four hours.

"Don't let this all go to your heads," he said, finally. "Los Pagos is a long way from New York . . . a long way from home."

III

They decided to celebrate their successful meeting in Stillwell's office by making reservations for dinner at a restaurant Harriet had seen reviewed in *The New York Times,* Lutèce.

A cordial host escorted Bunny and Harriet past the open kitchen where white-aproned chefs efficiently worked, past the dome-lighted garden room and up the stairs where they were soon seated at a corner table in a small, elegant dining room. Tapestries in softly muted earth tones adorned the walls. Gold threads shimmered in the tapestry on the wall nearest the fireplace. In the light cast by a cheering fire, Harriet observed a medieval hunting scene of birds in flight over a flaxen field.

"We're going first class tonight, Bunny. We'll have the best. Let's begin with champagne."

"The best? Mr. and Mrs. Pearl have always enjoyed Dom Perignon," Bunny said with a triumphant smile. "Do they have it?"

"Oh yes," Harriet said, "at a hundred and fifty dollars a bottle. What do you think?"

"I think you need to see the wine steward."

"And when Victor sees the bills for this dinner?"

"We'll be in Los Pagos, darling."

Bunny, turning her attention back to the menu, didn't notice that Harriet was blushing. Relieved, Harriet adjusted the knot of her tie and opened her menu.

"This food's a little on the exotic side, don't you think?" she asked, feeling a bit out of her element and wondering if she had made the best choice for their celebration dinner.

"It just sounds more exotic in French. Like everything else," Bunny said, a mischievous smile on her lips. "Read the English translation. Besides, this was *your* idea, Harry."

"I know. I just need a few more minutes to absorb the . . . ambience," she replied. "Anyway, I'm glad you're in such high spirits tonight."

"Who wouldn't be? Think of what our lives were like a few weeks ago and look at us now! We're decked out in designer clothes, we're staying at the very hotel where Bobby Short—in person—plays piano, and now we're about to dine in one of New York's most elegant restaurants. Don't be intimidated by *anything* tonight. Enjoy!"

Bunny's enthusiasm was infectious. "All right, I will," Harriet said emphatically. She looked at the menu, smiled agreeably and said, "I'll have shrimp terrine as an appetizer. And you?"

44

"Escargots, Harry, snails on a bed of puff pastry," Bunny whispered. "Positively wicked, don't you think?"

"What about the main course?"

"Fresh salmon with sorrel," Bunny replied, leaning back in her chair to look at Harriet. "And what will you have, Harry Pearl?"

"Rack of lamb, Bunny. With baby parsnips."

Still feeling the heady flush of the day's success, they were in the mood to linger over dessert. As Harriet cut into a slice of dark chocolate cake laced with brandy marinated apricots, she looked at Bunny, whose cheeks were aglow in the soft candlelight.

"Too bad we have to get back for Warren Bragg's phone call. I'm beginning to enjoy this place," Harriet said.

"Sort of grows on you, doesn't it? Try this," Bunny said, offering Harriet a taste of her Grand Marnier souffle.

Harriet was about to take the spoon from Bunny, but Bunny shook her head and fed Harriet the last of her dessert.

Outside the restaurant, Harriet enjoyed the smoky hint of autumn in the air. She would have liked to walk back to the hotel, but they couldn't miss the phone call, so she flagged a cab and soon they were back in their room. Not about to end the evening's festivities, Harriet called room service and ordered Courvoisier and coffee. She took off her shoes, sat on the sofa and stretched her long trousered legs on the velvet ottoman.

"This is the life, isn't it? Fine food, wonderful clothes, the best cigars. What more could a man ask for?"

Slipping into a robe, Bunny wondered about Harriet. She really *is* getting into this, she thought. I hope she's able to shift gears back into neutral when this assignment's over.

"Is something the matter?" Harriet inquired. "Did I say

something wrong? Don't you like the good life anymore?"

"Very much. I just wish we could give this role-playing a break now and then."

With a flourish, Harriet's finger crossed her lips and she whispered, "Ssssshhh."

"Oh Harriet, we took the bug out," Bunny said impatiently. "Don't you remember?"

"Then let's put it back in," Harriet said, ignoring her tone. "I know Victor will want to hear what we say to Bragg when he calls."

A short time later, they were speaking to him. He suggested they meet at the Garden Tea Room for lunch, a location convenient to their hotel. The tables on the patio were spaciously arranged, he said, there was no chance of being overheard.

As Harriet walked with Bunny out to the brick courtyard patio looking for the agent from Washington, knowing Bragg hadn't been told that she was a woman, she couldn't help wondering if she'd be able to pull it off.

Seated at a table at the edge of the patio, Warren Bragg stood and introduced himself to the Pearls. He shook Harriet's hand and then, with expansive gestures, pulled out a chair for Bunny. Harriet sat down, crossed her right ankle over her left knee and smiled confidently. He didn't suspect a thing, she decided.

Quickly, the Washington agent reviewed their plans for the coming weeks. Turner was giving a cocktail party that Friday night.

"You'll be my guests," he said. "I'm having lunch with Turner tomorrow. I'll tell him enough about you so you won't be complete strangers when you meet. You, Bunny," he continued, "have your heart set on carving a niche in the New York social scene. Harry, you are always willing to oblige the missus. I'll let Turner know that money is no object."

"Of course," Harriet said, in as deep a voice as she could muster and with a trace of irritation; she and Bunny were thoroughly familiar with these details.

Bunny smiled. At moments such as this, she couldn't help being amused by Harriet's intensity. She looked at Bragg who nodded to her as if acknowledging Bunny's smile as a gesture of affection and devotion to her husband.

It wasn't difficult to read his mind. She could tell he found her attractive—most men did. Yet she wasn't interested in even playfully pursuing the look she now saw in his eyes. Was this assignment getting the best of her as well, or was it that she found Harriet a much more appealing person than the beefy agent who sat across the table from her? She immediately dismissed the latter notion and poured herself more coffee from the small silver carafe.

Harriet, noting the agent's interest in Bunny, was annoyed. She frowned, then told herself to pay attention to business. Besides, why should she care if Bragg found Bunny attractive?

Once again Bragg reviewed their plans, then he asked for the check; and they soon parted company.

"Want anything else?" Harriet asked.

"No," Bunny said. 'Between digesting his master plan and that sandwich, I don't think I could take anything else."

"It gets pretty intense, doesn't it? We can't slip. Ever."

"It's harder for you, you were right about that," Bunny replied.

"Maybe," Harriet said. "But this is not going to be easy for either one of us. What do you say we take in a movie? I need a break, don't you?"

"I've got the perfect film—*Queen Christina* with Greta Garbo."

"With John Gilbert? What's so perfect about that?"

"She plays the role in drag—just like you, Harry—or at least she's dressed as a man for part of the film. It could be sort of like research for us."

"Gosh, Bunny, I said I need a break. Why don't we try a musical or a good suspense film?"

The movie, *North By Northwest*, succeeded in taking Harriet's mind off the assignment. Midway through the film, she leaned toward Bunny and said, "Got to go to the john . . . be right back."

"Don't forget to use the right one," Bunny whispered.

"Very funny."

The single stall in the men's room was occupied when Harriet walked in. After combing her hair and washing her hands, Harriet decided the stall's occupant must be reading a novel. How often was *this* going to happen? Absent-mindedly she gazed at the unfamiliar urinal perched midway up the opposite wall.

Eventually, an older gent carrying an umbrella emerged and ceremoniously announced, "It's all yours, my friend."

"Thanks," Harriet said, closing the door behind her.

Before she returned to the film, she looked in the mirror. She felt disturbed. She wanted Harriet back. "But Harriet's gone . . . or going," she said to her reflection. Then she returned to her seat and lost herself in darkness, figures on the screen taking her to worlds no stranger than the one she now inhabited.

Stepping out of the shower, Alan Turner reached for a bath towel and wrapped it around his waist. With the flat of his hand he wiped steam off the bathroom mirror, then flicked on the switch of his hair dryer; hot air flowed over his scalp as he brushed back thick, black hair.

At fifty-two, he was still a good-looking man. He worked out three mornings a week and the regimen achieved the effect he wanted: no sea of flab circled his muscular waist. In all ways, he thought, he projected the image of the foreign service, the diplomatic corps.

After receiving exceptionally high grades in the Foreign Service Officers' Exam, he had completed his training with one thought in mind: to culminate his career with an assignment as American Ambassador to a major world power. Yet after twenty-five years he had never achieved more than routine success as Consul in a series of posts such as the one he held in Venezuela.

I'm taking the future into my own hands now, he repeated to himself. I want more than a condo in the Florida sun and a government pension when I retire. I'm not married to the diplomatic corps . . . any more than I'm married to Bess Turner.

I never should have divorced her, he thought bitterly. For what? To save what she called her "pride?" Well, that's what she got—and with it she took her fortune, our children, and left me . . . what? A ledger filled with broken promises and debts.

And a desk full of dreams, he thought, his mood suddenly changing as he remembered the couple Warren Bragg had told him about. He'd be bringing them here tonight. Turner mused on the possibilities they presented. Warren said they'd helped him out when he needed funds a few years back. With no questions asked.

He'd been told that the high society of their home town, Cleveland, didn't want them. New York? New York was too fickle—it spat out Harry Pearls every day of the week.

I can offer them what I think they want. A place in the sun of Los Pagos.

Alan threw the towel into the hamper and jauntily walked into his bedroom to dress.

"El Sol de Los Pagos," he said aloud, envisioning the casino General José Hosada would soon build along the southern coast of the island.

He had finally persuaded the General that the casino was needed to put Los Pagos on the map. Aruba, St. Maarten, Antigua . . . Those islands had long ago established their gambling clientele; now it was time for Los Pagos to join their ranks. And *this* casino would put any in existence to shame.

Won't that make the old man happy, he asked himself. You're stubborn, Hosada, like the burros that graze on your palace grounds.

At first, the General had refused to listen to the merits of a casino. He was suspicious of outsiders wanting to establish a foothold on the island, mistrustful of the ambitions of foreigners. Turner had stressed that the establishment of the casino itself would provide Hosada with the necessary funds to maintain as strong a military police as he desired.

"Besides," Turner had told him, "the investors we choose will have no interest in the politics of the island. They'll be too busy making money for you—and for themselves, of course."

But the General had been skeptical, refusing to grant authority to invite willing investors to the island. It was Turner's persistence that had finally turned the tide. As part of his plan, he had become a willing admirer of the General's wife Maria. And he had offered his assistance and CIA contacts in securing mercenaries to train the island's military force, as well as aid in buying arms and munitions.

50

He had flattered Hosada into believing that his interests in helping Los Pagos were because of his personal admiration for the General and the General's ability to maintain peace on this tiny island for nearly three decades. For himself he would accept no more than a generous finder's fee.

But in fact he had been trying to interest a major gambling cartel in the island nation. He knew there was considerable interest in Los Pagos, but investors were hesitant because of the General's age.

"Once he passes on," Turner had been told, "who knows what will happen?"

But Turner had convinced them that Hosada would present no problems, that he was intent on establishing his succession and the permanency of his government. By finding investors for one new casino, the gambling cartel would follow. Then, as an investor in the cartel himself, he would reap great profits. It didn't matter whether Hosada ruled or Eduardo Gomez, his heir apparent; the potential for tremendous wealth was there.

Turner smiled as he thought of the General's wife, Maria. Hosada had already decreed that she would marry Eduardo upon the General's death.

I suppose I can live with that, he thought. Maria—you're everything Bess Turner wasn't, aren't you, my lovely? You're just what I need right now . . . and we're certainly compatible enough bedfellows.

"Don't stay away too long," Maria had said before he had left the island last month, "I will miss you too much. I can't bear to be missing you, Alan."

He knew what her words communicated. Maria would not be alone for long. She had told him that the General had long ago accepted what she described as her passionate nature. Her husband understood her appetites, her zest for life, but had told her that she should choose her companions carefully. He naively believed that on Los Pagos everything was brought to his attention.

Turner learned very quickly that nothing was brought to the General's attention unless it had previously received Maria's approval.

And though the old man seemed to be interested in nothing more than assuring Maria that she would always live in a style befitting a General's wife, she had ambitious plans for social programs that would benefit the islanders. The General needed new sources of revenue to carry out these plans, but who was willing to take on an aged dictator as a business partner? With luck, Turner thought, it will be the Pearls.

Turner smiled, thinking of the lavish attention Maria gave the islanders and her many stories of the children, the ones she seemed to love the most. She was happiest when she was holding babies in her arms or escorting young boys and girls through the Market Square as they made their way to the small schoolhouse under the shade of the tall palm trees near the presidential Palace.

From her perspective, the Casino would bring great riches to the natives of her island. She knew Los Pagos could not secure its future through its outmoded sugar factories, the sporadic catches of its fishing fleet, or its fitful tourist trade.

He recalled her parting words: "One day my sweet Alan, when Papa goes to his well-deserved resting place, all will know that you are my special one."

He smiled again. We're a winning combination now, Maria, but don't be too sure of more than that.

Bunny and Harriet had spent much of the afternoon deciding on what they would wear to Alan Turner's cocktail party. Since their first shopping spree, Harriet had added two more suits to her wardrobe. She'd chosen her newest purchase for this evening's affair, a soft grey worsted cut in the latest European fashion, along with an off-white shirt and a pearl grey tie embossed with thin stripes of midnight blue.

"Seen my black alligator shoes anywhere?" Harriet asked as she bent over and looked under the sofa.

"No," Bunny said, "but wear a pair of mine. Maybe it's just the final touch you need."

"Cute. You're still ticked off about this afternoon, aren't you?" Harriet stood, a shoe in each hand.

"What if I am?" she asked indignantly. "What gave you the right to barge into Gregor's the way you did?"

"You said you'd be through by three, it was almost four when I dropped by. What *is* the big deal?"

"Men don't come after their wives when they're having their hair done!"

"You talk about me and this role-playing. You should have seen yourself today when I—"

"The only thing I know is that Gregor's hands were trembling for the rest of the appointment. He's told me he doesn't like to be interrupted for *any* reason. And when you lit up one of your cigars, I thought he was going to put me under the dryer just as I was."

"So?" Harriet said, amused that Bunny was still angry with her. "Bunny, come on, your hair's never looked better."

"You really think so?" Bunny asked. She touched her hair lightly, smiled at Harriet and looked in the mirror.

"Of course," Harriet confirmed, trying to suppress a smile as she thought how easy it was to pull Bunny out of her moods with a bit of flattery.

"Do you think I look all right for the party?" Bunny asked quietly.

"You look beautiful," Harriet said sincerely, "you really do. You know, I feel as if I'm going to my coming-out party. I just don't think I look, well, manly enough."

"You look gentle," Bunny said softly, "that's a nice way for a man to look."

"Think we're going to do all right tonight?"

Bunny smiled. "Like charms."

Victor Stillwell had spent hours listening to the tapes from Bunny and Harriet's hotel room. At no time did they ever talk like anyone but Mr. and Mrs. Pearl from Cleveland, Ohio.

Those dames have gone over the hill, he thought. The only thing they aren't doing is having sex.

He tapped his pen on his desk and rewound the latest tape. Apparently Bunny had Harriet in tow; she was deferential to all of Bunny's commands. Strange birds, he thought.

That morning Warren Bragg had told him that he was optimistic that the Pearls would make the necessary connection with Turner. "It's only a matter of time now," Bragg had said.

"You actually think this Harry Pearl and Bunny Silver make a convincing husband and wife team?"

"Sure do," Warren said. "When I've seen them together, Harry can't take his *eyes* off Bunny. I think he's going to have problems letting her go when this assignment's over."

"What about Bunny?" Victor asked, "How's she coming across?"

"The doting wife if there ever was one. You know, as

far as assignments go, I envy Harry Pearl. Bunny is one nice handful of woman."

"Put the move on her then. She's not married to Harry Pearl. This is just a routine assignment."

"Don't think I haven't made a try or two with that doll, but she's got eyes for no one but Pearl."

"That so?" Victor had asked feeling an odd twinge of jealousy. What a joke, he thought, wait until Bragg finds out Harry's a dame. He'd like to tell him right now, but Sam Perry had insisted that he didn't want any details to leak before the case was resolved.

As the Pearls stepped from the elevator into the lobby of The Carlyle, they saw Warren Bragg waiting for them.

"Bunny," he called, "good evening. Harry, how's it going?"

"Fine, Warren," Harriet said, her voice falling to a lower register than usual, which often happened when she was nervous.

"You're right on time, you two," Warren said. "Let's catch a cab. We'll be at Turner's hotel in no time at all." Then, feeling the Pearls' tension, Warren said, "We just got to play it loose."

"Easier said than done," replied Harriet.

"Come on," Warren said, "your cover's airtight."

"Of course it is," Bunny responded, taking Harriet's hand in her own. "Harry's just had a bad day, haven't you, dear?"

"Is that what it is?" Harriet said wryly.

A few minutes later Alan Turner welcomed Bragg and his companions, ushering them into his tastefully decorated suite. The living room was crowded with Turner's guests, and after making a few introductions, Turner excused himself and disappeared into the crowd. But Harriet was aware that no matter where Turner stood, his eyes were on the two of them.

Harriet had to concede that Bunny had really come into her own. She circulated constantly, introducing herself and Harriet to everyone she met. She was the image of the Midwestern matron she was supposed to be, and Harriet had no choice but to play the role of the devoted husband, joining her and her new acquaintances in small talk as she was drawn into the conversation.

Turner had already ordered his own contacts to thoroughly check out the Pearls, but from all that he observed, it seemed unlikely there would be any problems. The party was drawing to a close when he walked over to Warren Bragg and the Pearls.

"I apologize," he said, "I haven't been much of a host to you and your wife. By any chance are you free for lunch tomorrow?"

"Are we?" Bunny asked, turning to Harriet.

"For the Consul, of course we are."

"My pleasure," Turner replied. "Warren tells me you're staying at The Carlyle. Suppose I call for you at noon?"

"Wonderful," Harriet answered.

"And thank you so much for the delightful party," Bunny said, tremors of excitement in her voice. "We met so *many* interesting people, Mr. Turner."

Turner laughed and put an arm around each of them. "Isn't that what parties are for?"

Outside Turner's hotel, Warren clapped Harriet on the shoulder.

"And you were worried, Harry! What did I tell you? You two pulled this off just the way I knew you would. How about the three of us stopping off for a celebration drink?"

"Thanks all the same, Warren," Harriet said, "but there's something I want to do with Bunny right now. I'm afraid three would make a crowd."

"Why, Harry Pearl," Bunny exclaimed, "what *do* you have on your mind? What a devil he is, Warren. Being in New York just brings out the beast in him. And don't I *love* it!"

Warren and Bunny laughed. Harriet looked up toward Central Park.

"We're going for a carriage ride," Harriet said, "it's something I've always wanted to do."

Bragg smiled at Harry Pearl. "All right, you two," he said, "the night's still young. I'll phone tomorrow . . . after your lunch with Turner."

As Bunny and Harriet walked up 5th Avenue, Bunny said, "This is something I've always wanted to to, too, but I never thought I was elegant enough. And the guys I've dated—forget it. Why take a ride through Central Park, when Monday Night Football's on? Know what I mean? Nice enough guys, I guess—just not romantic. A woman *wants* romance. At least once in her life."

"Bunny, you look elegant enough tonight for anything," Harriet said.

As they strolled toward the waiting carriages, Harriet stopped at a small pushcart and bought Bunny a long-stemmed rose. "For romance," she said. "Once in your life."

They were quiet on their ride through the park. Bunny held her rose in her hands, Harriet looked out at the night.

Bunny broke the silence. "What do you think of our new friend?"

"He's clever," Harriet replied. "He'll do his homework on us between now and tomorrow, but our story will check."

For a time, there was no further conversation between the two. Through the trees, Harriet looked up at the heavens, bright stars shining in the night.

I'm Harry Pearl, she thought. But if I *am,* where did Harriet go? How did I lose her so quickly?

Harriet knew, then, that Bunny was a large part of the answer to her question. Suddenly, she trembled; she wanted to block what was becoming clear to her.

"Are you cold?" Bunny asked.

"Cold," Harriet repeated. "No, I was just thinking of something, Bunny."

"This is a nice place to think."

She looked at Harriet. Harry Pearl, she said to herself, you're turning into that dream I've spent my whole life looking for. What would you say if I told you that? Not that I'm about to say a word—we're on this crazy assignment now and if Victor has a chance to pull the rug out from under our feet he will. Who knows what it's going to be like when we get to Los Pagos? Not to mention what could happen between now and when we do get there. Still, when it's all over, if it's the success we both want it to be, we'll finally be full-fledged agents. Maybe then we can say goodbye to Victor Stillwell. And Mr. and Mrs. Pearl as well, she thought with regret.

Ah, don't ruin the evening, she told herself, enjoy what your mother's always wanted for you: a romantic husband. And you're on a secret assignment to boot. Who said dreams don't come true?

IV

In the weeks that followed, Turner and the Pearls were constant companions. Bunny was sympathetic when Turner talked about his marriage and divorce and appropriately in awe of his stories of life in the diplomatic service—and on Los Pagos.

"And you two," he had asked early in their relationship, "what brings you all the way to New York?"

"Lately, Alan, Cleveland's seemed like a mighty small town," Harriet replied. "Our major investments were in steel. I'm sure you know the sorry fate of that industry in the Midwest. All over the state, the mills shut down . . . a disaster. We were lucky enough to bail out in time."

"Good for you," Turner said in a chipper tone of voice.

"I'll say, but the change in the financial picture wasn't

59

the only consideration. For some reason, Alan, though Bunny and I donated small fortunes to the Symphony and the Art Museum, we never felt we were part of the inner circle."

"Harry," Bunny said, "that sounds depressing."

"Goodness, yes," Turner said brightly, "cheer up. New York's different. With the correct, shall we say, sponsor, you'll have no trouble meeting someone to provide the necessary entrée into any circle you desire."

"I hope you're right," Harriet said. "That's why we came east, Alan."

"And New York *is* exciting," Bunny said. "The parties you've taken us to . . . the people we've met—"

"We've enjoyed ourselves, haven't we?" Turner asked cordially. "I'm not embarrassed to say that I'm going to miss you nice people."

"Miss us?" Bunny asked. "What do you mean? We're not going anywhere."

"Ah, but I am, dear. For personal reasons," he said in a tone of confidentiality, "I've taken an extended leave of absence from my post in Caracas."

"I didn't know that," she said sympathetically.

"Yes," he continued, "I need time to myself now—away from official responsibilities. I'm taking a peaceful and indefinite holiday on the beautiful island of Los Pagos. But that still gives us a few more days to take New York by storm."

Bunny pouted and rubbed her hands together anxiously. "New York's too big," she said, "we don't really have any friends here."

"Bunny," Harriet said, a stern reprimand in her voice, "we're not children. We'll make friends. After all, life isn't one big cotillion. Besides, it's time I paid attention to these new investments. They're not going to take care of themselves, you know."

"Oh, Harry, I just want us to have fun. You've said yourself you could take care of business anywhere in the world you could plug in your computer."

Harriet laughed self-consciously. "All right, Bunny, you win that one."

Turner reached across the table for the bottle of chilled Muscadet they were enjoying with their lunch. "If what you say is true, we *do* have electricity in Los Pagos. Why don't you fly down with me next week and I'll introduce you to General Hosada and his lovely wife Maria?"

"You don't mean it!" Bunny exclaimed.

"Why wouldn't I?" he said in a jovial voice. "What do you say, Harry?"

Harriet shook her head no. "Bunny, we'll stay where we are. We have our itinerary all planned for the next few weeks."

"I understand, Harry," Turner replied. "But I want you to know that the invitation is a standing one. Come down any time. I am sorry, however, that you can't join us on this particular trip. The Swans are coming with me. Last year they built a home on Los Pagos ... a charming place."

"Do you mean *the* John Swan?" Bunny asked, her voice rising with excitement.

"None other," Turner said.

"Oh, Harry," Bunny said, in a pleading voice, "we'll never have a chance like this again."

Harriet looked from Turner to Bunny and then back again. "It's that important to you, isn't it, darling?" Harriet asked. "Then we'll go. Alan, we'll be pleased to join you."

Bunny smiled. "Harry, you're such a dear."

"I'd say this calls for a toast," Turner said, raising his wine glass.

The Pearls met with Warren Bragg the next morning to tell him of the planned trip to Los Pagos.

"Wasn't difficult to get him to take the bait, was it?" Warren asked in a confident voice.

Bunny laughed. "Not at all. I'm just *ever* so anxious to fly to Los Pagos with the Swans. Poor Harry couldn't have said no if he'd wanted to."

"Easy, eh, Harry?" Warren asked.

"You might say that," Harriet answered, lighting a cigar.

The three of them were in good humor. They began to discuss how they would encourage Turner to invite them to invest in his financial project with the Hosadas.

"Take it slowly . . . there's no rush," Warren said. "Give yourselves a chance to get a feel for the island. For Turner. For the General. For Maria Hosada. We'll take all the time we need to reel in this baby."

"And when will we meet again?" Bunny asked, flirting for just a second with Agent Bragg. "Or is this our New York adios?"

"Didn't Stillwell tell you?" Bragg asked. "You're going on alone. There was a possiblity that I'd be joining you, but Sam Perry was so impressed with the two of you that he didn't think my assistance was necessary. And it isn't. I've got as much confidence in your abilities as Perry does. We'll meet again, though . . . let's say the day after tomorrow. Same time. Same place."

One more time, Victor Stillwell reviewed the details and agenda of the Turner case for Warren Bragg, as Bragg, sitting across the desk from his senior agent, doodled idly on a yellow legal pad.

As Stillwell bent his crew-cut head over the sheaf of papers, his blunt skull suggested the persistent strength of a battering ram. He was prepared to push long and hard enough against any obstacle until it gave way to his demands.

What should have been a brief, routine review was turning into a lengthy examination of each step of the operation. In searching for any possible weaknesses in the plan, Stillwell grew more and more agitated, then realized he would have been in better spirits if the Pearls had failed to hook Turner.

Suddenly Stillwell sat upright in his chair and crossed his left leg over his right. In his hand he held a judge's gavel; the hard polished mahogany gleamed in the morning sunlight that flickered into the room. As he reiterated the major points of the plan, he tapped the gavel against his artificial leg.

Bragg had been told about this odd habit of Stillwell's. As he tried to respond, each mention by him of Pearl or Silver brought a tapping of Stillwell's gavel against his prosthesis.

"I think they're damn good agents," Warren said. "You don't have a thing to worry about."

"Is that so?" Stillwell spat back in a voice thick with anger, his gavel hammering. "Nobody asked you what you think about them."

Bragg looked at Stillwell but made no reply.

"We don't want to waste time," Stillwell continued. "As soon as Pearl and Silver come up with any hard evidence against Turner, we'll move in fast."

"As you say, Victor."

Stillwell thumped his leg one last time. "On target," he said. Impertinent bastard, Victor thought as Warren left his office.

From the top dresser drawer, Bunny unfolded one of Harriet's new polo shirts.

"Wear this tonight," she said, "you can show off your muscles."

Harriet turned, took Bunny's hand and ran it down her arm. "I don't have muscles," she said.

"No . . . your arms are soft . . . like they should be." Then Bunny's tone lightened as she said, "I was teasing you."

"I know," Harriet said gently.

There was an awkward tension between the two women, then in a playful gesture Bunny squeezed Harriet's arm. She was tempted to give her a kiss on the cheek, but she stepped back and walked to a nearby window. Looking out on the scene below, she reflected that it was getting harder and harder to realize that Harry was Harriet.

Thoughts raced through her mind. Who am I falling for anyway? Harry Pearl—who doesn't really exist? Or Harriet? If it's Harriet, what in the hell does that mean? But it's as if Harriet just isn't here. If she isn't, then *who* is Harry?"

"Too much!" Bunny exclaimed aloud.

"What's that?" Harriet asked.

"Nothing. Just put on your shirt and let's go out for a bite to eat."

The morning they were to leave for Los Pagos, Alan Turner met the Pearls in the lobby of their hotel. He was all smiles as he walked toward them.

"Bunny, Harry," he exclaimed as he reached out to embrace them, "we are about to begin a trip I promise you will not forget. To begin, we are flying to Los Pagos on the Swan's private plane."

"We are? That's *so* exciting," Bunny said, linking her arm with Turner's. "I just couldn't sleep a *wink* last night. Poor Harry, I must have been up a dozen times. I wanted to be absolutely *sure* that I'd packed every single thing I had on my list."

"Then let me help you," Turner said, picking up her heavy tote bag.

"I'll take that, Alan," Harriet said, hoisting the bag over her shoulder. "There's no telling what Bunny packed in here at the last minute."

Turner laughed. "My driver's put the rest of your luggage in the car. He's waiting out front for us."

John and Adeline Swan were already at the airport when Turner and the Pearls arrived. Their sleek Gulfstream IV was ready for takeoff at Runway 19, and as they all walked in that direction, Bunny couldn't help giving Harry an excited squeeze.

"We're on our way," she said, "we're actually on our way."

"What I wouldn't give to have Victor see us now," Harriet whispered as she took Bunny's arm.

The Swans were cordial hosts to Bunny and Harriet, though their demeanor was predictably cool and reserved.

Typical, Bunny thought. Who are we to them but two social climbers from Cleveland, while they go wherever they want on their own private jet. From the looks of the kitchen, they could invite Julia Child on board as their personal chef. They probably have a yacht, too. Wonder what their place on Los Pagos is like?

She turned in Turner's direction and said softly, "Will our accommodations be near Mr. and Mrs. Swan's?"

Turner chuckled. "Not exactly. They've built their home at the western tip of Los Pagos but I'm sure you'll be having cocktails there before the week's out."

Bunny turned to Harriet. "Harry," she said, "did you hear?"

As the cruising altitude was reached, the small party of five passengers relaxed. The Swans, sitting in comfortable leather chairs, were engaged in quiet conversation with each other. Harriet looked out on a beautiful sky, reached for a cigar, lit up and said, "Bunny, all your dreams are going to come true."

Soon after breakfast was served, Turner requested that the first bottle of a case of champagne he'd had brought on board be served.

"It's never too early for champagne on Los Pagos, so let's enjoy some refreshments on our way to this beautiful island."

The steward raised two folded teak tables, inserted silver ice buckets in place, and then filled the crystal champagne glasses. Soon, even the Swans began to appreciate the holiday spirit Turner was so intent on maintaining, though it wasn't long before the silver-haired John Swan closed his eyes and dozed.

Harriet was sitting next to Turner on a custom-built grey leather sofa; it ran a good fourteen feet down one side of the plane, which had been decorated in tones of powder blue and white. She began to chat with him about the gym facilities on Los Pagos, telling him she was intent on maintaining a daily exercise program.

"The General has one of the finest gyms you're likely to see," Turner said expansively. "The pool is Olympic size, I swim each morning—why don't you join me?"

"Swim," Harriet said, her voice suddenly hoarse. "Oh, no swimming for me, Alan. I've got swimmer's ear. Weights, that's my specialty."

For a slim guy, Turner thought, he's sure not lifting much in the weight department, but if that's what keeps him happy, I'll make sure the weights he needs are there.

Harriet turned in Bunny's direction. The steward was bending over her in a way that Harriet didn't like.

"Bunny," Harriet called, to get her attention.

"Yes, dear," Bunny replied, "come join us. Juan's been reading my palm. It's fascinating. He sees a great adventure in my future, much success . . . "

"And romance," the steward said, turning to face Harriet. "Much, much romance. I think your wife is a passionate woman."

Speechless for a second, Harriet nudged Turner and said, "And you think I don't know that? Any more champagne, steward?" She raised her empty glass.

Seated next to Bunny again, Harriet said in a low voice, "Stop flirting. Mrs. Swan's already loking down her nose at the neckline of your dress—"

"Where do you get off?" Bunny asked, suddenly angry. "Flirting! That's not all I should do. A few more weeks of this—"

"More champagne, Bunny," Harriet said in a loud, cheery voice. "It's a long flight, darling. Bunny, do you hear me? It's a long flight." She leaned over Bunny and whispered. "When we get to Los Pagos, I may not always be with you. We can't risk any slipups. What's happening to you?"

Bunny said, "It's the champagne . . . I never could drink more than a glass."

"Then switch to coffee," Harriet said, "or take a nap."

"Damn," Bunny muttered to herself. "Damn it."

67

"It's all right," Harriet whispered, "Don't be angry with yourself. Turner's busy chatting with Mrs. Swan now. No one heard us—"

"I think I will take a nap. Wake me when we're about to land. I want to put on fresh makeup and comb my hair. Are you mad at me, Harry?" she asked.

"No, I'm not mad, but we can't relax our guard for a minute. For all we know, that steward's working for Turner."

"You're right. How could I have been so stupid?" She snuggled down into her seat. "I just need a little nap, Harry."

"Sweet dreams," she said, as Bunny closed her eyes.

When the approach to Los Pagos was announced, Harriet leaned across the still sleeping Bunny and looked out the window. Beneath a bank of hazy clouds, she saw the clear water of the Caribbean, the surf a chain of turquoise gems breaking on smooth white sand. Then, as the plane veered sharply to the right, the glare from the bright afternoon sun blocked her view. Los Pagos, she thought, are you really down there?

The plane began its final descent and off in the distance, Harriet saw what looked like nothing more than a speck in the sea. We're going to land on *that*, she thought.

"We're almost there, Harry," Turner called back. "Aren't you going to wake Bunny? Landing on the island is an experience in itself. I don't think she'll want to miss it."

I sure wish I could, Harriet thought. Better wake her, though. We need a few minutes to synchronize our gears. Gently, Harriet shook Bunny's shoulder.

"Later," Bunny said. "Let me alone. I want to sleep."

"Bunny, come on," Harriet said. "We're directly over Los Pagos. Take a look, come on. Don't you want to comb your hair, fix your makeup?"

"Buzz off," Bunny mumbled.

Harriet shook her arm, sat her up in the seat. "Rise and shine my little sunbeam. Come *on*, Bunny. Take a look at the place, for God's sake."

"All right, all right," she said, sitting up and glaring out the window. When she spotted the island, she looked at Harriet and said, "Oh, no, I don't even have a will."

"Neither do I," Harriet said morosely.

"Most unique airfield in the world," Turner informed them. "See that narrow valley between those two mountains? We cut in there, shave a few tree tops off on the way, bounce down the field and if we're lucky the pilot will stop this worthy craft before we skid into the sea. Say your prayers, Pearls. I always do before landing on Los Pagos."

"He's not kidding, is he?" Bunny muttered.

Harriet shook her head and gripped the arms of her chair. Then she shut her eyes and did as she'd been told. She said her prayers.

"Oh, Harry, Loooook," Bunny squealed, grabbing Harriet's arm. "It's beautiful." Then, kissing Harriet on the cheek, she whispered, "Open your eyes you coward and look out the window."

The plane seemed to be hovering above the island but as they looked below they could both see the valley which separated the two tallest mountain peaks. Then the plane dropped and instead of the blueness of the sky, Bunny looked out on the lush green forests of Los Pagos.

"Why are we doing this?" she asked.

"You wanted to get out of Cleveland. Remember?"

The impact of the landing itself was sudden. Wheels struck the tarmac runway, wing-flaps reversed and over the speaker of the plane the rousing strains of a military march were heard.

"The National Anthem of Los Pagos," Turner said. "The General insists that it be played at both landings and takeoffs. I am sure the Swans don't ordinarily adhere to this custom, but it was thoughtful of them to do so today."

"Don't tell me we have to stand at attention," Harriet commented dourly.

"Not on this occasion," Turner said, "but otherwise, yes. You'll come to recognize the song quickly, you'll hear it everywhere on the island. 'Los Pagos, Star of the Sea.' Maria Hosada is the composer of the anthem. I'll see that you receive a copy of the lyrics. They're quite stirring. Patriotism is always at the forefront of life on Los Pagos."

The plane stopped none too soon for either Harriet or Bunny. As they stepped forward, the steward opened the door and fastened the clamp of the stair ramp to the body of the Gulfstream jet. Waves of Los Pagos heat seemed to engulf the plane. Instinctively, Bunny stepped back but the steward took her arm and encouraged her descent. Turner stood beside them as they looked at the desolate strip of land, the three aluminum hangars, the stark cinder block office of the Los Pagos airport.

"Don't judge the island by this airfield," he said. "It's scheduled for major renovations within the next few years. Until now, there hasn't been an overabundance of air traffic to and from the island—many tourists come here by ship. Things will change, though. Progress will stamp its mark even on Los Pagos. Reserve judgment until you've seen the beautiful beaches, the fishing villages, the General's home. Your accommodations are quite charming," he continued, "as you'll soon see."

Then they heard a low humming noise in the distance. Through clouds of dust, they could see a military jeep followed by what appeared to be a vintage white Cadillac convertible. The car swerved dangerously to the left and passed the jeep, leaving it behind in the dust. As the Cadillac approached the small group which had just left the plane, Harriet saw a swirl of golden hair caught up by the wind, and a bare arm, bejeweled and braceleted, waving. The driver slammed on the brakes of the car only seconds before the group began to scatter in front of it.

The car door opened and onto the dusty tarmac stepped the woman. A heady perfume filled the air.

"Alan! You're back . . . you're back on Los Pagos," she called, rushing toward Turner, embracing him without a thought to the others standing near him. Her kisses were sudden, passionate. Just as abruptly as she had greeted him, she pulled back, spun around and faced the group.

"Señora Maria Theresa Annuciata Hosada at your service, my beloved guests. Welcome to our friendly island. Los Pagos, Star of the Sea."

She reached out for Alan's hand and held it as if it were her dearest treasure. "Alan, Alan, Alan," she murmured in soft tones, "Maria has missed you so."

Turner tried to preserve his diplomatic demeanor, but with Maria hanging onto his arm, twisting his fingers in her hands, whispering words of deep affection, it was obviously difficult.

Harriet and Bunny exchanged looks that registered their incredulity. Mesmerized by Maria's display, John Swan appeared to be riveted to the dusty terrain. Adeline Swan turned away and walked back in the direction of the plane.

"John, let me know when Armando arrives," she called in a sharp voice.

"Yes dear," he answered, "momentarily, I'm sure."

"I think it's best we remain in the plane until he arrives," she said loftily. "I don't intend to be a part of this . . . "

A car was rapidly approaching, a thick cloud of dust in its wake.

"Armando's here, Adeline, we'll be home in minutes."

With a cool nod at Maria Hosada, Adeline Swan walked off the airfield, her hand securely on her husband's arm. No other farewells had been spoken.

Harriet stared at Maria Hosada. Though she was voluptuous, the word itself wasn't adequate to describe her. She was tall. Her hair was a thick golden mane. Her dark brown eyes sparkled with glints of gold. Her lips were full; pouting was their natural expression. Her breasts, overly exposed in the flowered sundress she wore, invited admiration. She wore exotic makeup, expensive jewelry—rings on every finger and heavy, dangling gold earrings that swayed back and forth against her neck as she laughed or shook her head or emitted an expression of pleasure at having Turner in her midst once more.

And then she saw Harry Pearl.

"Introduce me to your new friends, Alan," she said in a throaty growl. "Introduce me to our American visitors."

She left Turner's side and stepped to Harriet. She extended her hand, looked her straight in the eye and said in a low voice, "Hello, USA."

Harriet wasn't prepared for this. She looked down at her shoes. Maria reached out for her hand and held it in a firm embrace.

Turner made the introductions, bringing Bunny forward; but the small woman standing next to this tall, handsome, fair-haired man obviously didn't interest Maria in the least.

"We will have a chance to talk tonight," Maria said. "The General is taking his nap right now, but I want you to come to the Palace for dinner. Eight o'clock, Harry Pearl."

She turned to walk toward her car, then looked back at

Turner. "Call me when your guests are settled, Alan."

"The Señora," Turner explained, "the General's wife, is enthusiastic about greeting newcomers to the island. It means nothing."

But Harriet knew better.

V

Maria burst into the General's bedroom. She threw herself against the bulk of his large body and whistled lightly in his ear.

"Papa," she whispered, "our investors are here. Wake up, I have much to tell you."

The General responded with a grunt.

"General Hosada. Attention . . . it's time to review the guards."

Hosada's eyelids fluttered; then lizard fashion they opened quickly and he looked up at his wife. "Do not mislead me in this fashion. I have reviewed the troops today. It is not something which I take lightly."

"Oh, Papa, I wanted to bring you back from dreamland.

I have exciting news. Our problems are soon to be solved
... just as Alan said."

The General looked at Maria with detachment. "I'm
listening," he said as he yawned and stretched in his
king-sized bed.

The General's hair and beard were snowy white, his
cheeks, nose and eyes were round, the bulk of his stomach
protruded under his nightshirt presenting the dimensions of
a gently rounded tent. Yet under the clinging silk sheet
which covered him, his legs were thin spindles barely able
to support his huge body. He struggled to sit up but Maria
stretched out over him, confining even his thin arms, his
arthritic hands.

"I am so happy," she said excitedly, "our dreams *will*
come true."

He grunted again, reached for his wife and pulled her
down on the bed beside him.

"Papa, this is no time for games," she said, humoring
him. "Don't you want to hear my news?" Affectionately,
she stroked his beard, twisting thin strands of hair around
her fingers.

"Of course, my darling," he replied, "but I also want
you next to me."

She told the story quickly, leaving her impression of
Harry Pearl for last. "He's sweet ... a shy man, Papa, fair
of skin, and oh so blond."

His eyes glimmered as he noted her enthusiasm for the
American investor. "Do not be too flirtatious, Maria," he
said with a stern note of caution in his voice. "His wife will
become jealous, and then we will never taste the fruits of
his fortune."

"I will be no more than hospitable—as the First Lady
of Los Pagos should be."

Maria's mind ran in its usual orderly fashion. It might be fun to uncouple Mr. USA from that wife of his but the General was right. The money came first ... then she would complete her plans for Los Pagos. She gazed at her husband with fondness.

"Papa, now that I have told you the news, I must make my daily confession to the blessed father."

"How long will you be gone?" he asked.

"Not long, the people are accustomed to seeing me in church each day. I must confess ... then I must pray. My soul must be pure," she said piously.

The General smiled. "The priest's soul must be pure as well, Maria, so don't tempt him in the confessional."

She laughed. "Papa, even as a young girl working in the sugar factory, I never fooled with the holy fathers, though there was one sweet young padre who ... ah, but that was so long ago." She bent down and kissed him goodbye. "But you, Papa, saved me from what would have been a life of poverty and travail ... Without you, what else would I have known? And with you, my General, I am Maria Hosada, First Lady of Los Pagos."

Turner had left the Pearls to unpack and settle in the charming guest house he promised would be their home for as long as they wanted to stay.

"Isn't this wonderful?" Bunny walked across the living room and looked up the stairs to the second floor. "It's so roomy ... so spacious and airy."

As Bunny spoke, Harriet made a quick search of the first floor for bugging devices. She found one at the base of a small table lamp.

"Come upstairs, let's look around before we unpack," Bunny said in a light, cheerful voice.

76

As they chatted in their bedroom, they found another bug which had been installed at the tip of a brass drapery rod. Then Bunny opened the French doors leading out to a small balcony. They searched the balcony and found nothing.

"At least we'll be able to talk out here," Harriet said.

"The bugs will come in handy," Bunny replied. "We'll be able to push Turner close to asking us for the money. Then we move in as agents and nab him for violating the diplomatic code by directly involving himself in the affairs of a foreign govenrment."

"You make it sound so easy," Harriet said. "We could run into trouble down here."

"We will, Harry, my darling. And it's going to begin as soon as Maria lets loose with her charm." Bunny laughed, "How are you going to resist her, Señor Pearl?"

"With a wife like you, it won't be any problem," Harriet answered. "Stay by my side and she won't stand a chance."

From their balcony, the surrounding waters sparkled like jewels in the afternoon sun. Along the beach children played, while in the harbor fishing boats bobbed up and down in the gentle swells. Tall palm trees surrounded the guest house and from these trees and the lush forest beyond came a swell of tropical sounds: insects, birds, a ceaseless cry and chatter that merged with the gentle surf that broke along the shore. Bunny looked at the flowers growing in large pots on the balcony. She picked a delicate pink blossom and inhaled the sweet aroma. "A vacation paradise isn't it, Harry?"

Harriet reached for Bunny's hand, realized what she was doing and stepped away, putting her own hands deep into the pockets of her trousers.

"All it needs is a casino," Harriet said in a matter-of-fact tone of voice, feeling troubled by these sudden impulses she had been feeling to express affection toward Bunny.

"They won't be able to keep the tourists away. It's a Caribbean gold mine," Bunny replied. "I'm feeling tired, Harry. I want to take a nap and feel fresh for the General's dinner party."

She turned and stepped back into their room.

Maria was dressing for the party when the General appeared at her door. His steps slow and unsteady, he reached for the bedpost, his hands shaking as he clutched the gleaming ebony. As he sat, he sighed.

"Maria, listen to me. Now. There is not much time that is left to me. I feel it—I know it, we must complete our goals soon."

Maria sat beside her husband, taking his gnarled hands in her own.

"Papa, we have years to be together. You've had these feelings before."

His voice was stern. "You humor me, that is all. You know I'm speaking the truth. You must be prepared to marry Eduardo when I die. Next to you, he is my most trusted friend, my ally. You and he will complete what I do not live to finish—"

"I can't allow you to talk this way," Maria said, taking the General's chin in her hand, turning his tired, old face to look at her. "Papa, I will not marry him. He is stupid, evil tempered, mean spirited—"

"It was all decided a long time ago," the General said patiently. "I have chosen him as my heir and you must stand at his side. He expects what he has earned, what has been promised to him."

"Have I ever questioned your decisions without good

reason?" Maria asked. "You must listen to me about Eduardo. I know what our island needs . . . I know what will carry it forward. This is what you want, isn't it? A vision for the future. Eduardo hasn't the strength to provide this—you know that. Why won't you listen to me? I will govern Los Pagos fairly, justly—"

"Enough foolishness, Maria. You are a woman. A very special woman, but not a man. You will carry on as First Lady."

Gently, Maria stroked his cheeks, brushed wisps of hair back from his bloodshot eyes. "You are always so sure that you are right, aren't you, Papa?"

She returned to her dressing table and in her mirror watched the aged Hosada lie back on her bed. As she completed her makeup, her mind raced.

She was determined to succeed her husband. She knew that the people of Los Pagos would accept her, that they would support her plans for the future. The General had not walked the village paths in years, but she had. He had lost touch with his people.

She brushed her thick hair quickly. I will never stand at Eduardo's side, she thought angrily. When the General is gone, I will govern alone.

She turned to look at her husband who had fallen into a deep sleep. Tenderly, she caressed his brow. Poor Papa, she thought, I know you would walk the dirt roads of our villages if you could, but you are too feeble to travel. Ah, in your time, you were followed from village to village, cheered everywhere you went.

And Eduardo? You do not know how lazy he is, how irresponsible, how much he drinks. He is too proud to consort with our people, he is only too content to sit behind that grand desk of his.

She smoothed the skirt of the dress she would wear

that evening. Men, she thought, they drive me crazy. The General wants this dictatorship to continue, Eduardo thinks he's next in line, Alan wants to control me as well as the resort ... Well, none will get their wish. We don't need iron rule. Under Maria, the winds of democracy will bring us forward—into this century. In a free election, the people will choose me.

So Alan cannot ask the Pearls for money directly, he must keep his hands clean. We must have money, though, and we will have the casino, even if it is to be a double-edged sword. Used properly, the profits will bring education to the young, medical care for the old.

Maria gazed at her reflection in the mirror, her thoughts turning to Harry Pearl.

What a sweet man he seems to be. I wonder what his interests are ... other than his wife and his fine fortune. If I can find some diversion for the wife, I may have a chance to entertain the husband.

As Maria considered the possibilities, the General began to groan in pain. Then, from the depths of his gargantuan stomach, he belched.

"Ah," he said contentedly, "the goat stew at lunch was spicier than usual ... but delicious."

Turner leaned back in his chair, listening to the Pearls as they dressed for dinner. He was aware that Maria found Harry attractive, but there was little risk that the American would capture her affections, at least not with Bunny watching over him. This was going to be easier than planned, he thought, chuckling at their idle banter.

"Harry, just think," Bunny was saying, "Alan is going to introduce us to so many society people—"

"Does that make you happy, darling?"

"You know damn well it does, sweets. With the right connections, we'll even be able to find a place for ourselves in New York. We might not go back to Ohio at all."

"Don't be so hasty, Bunny. Ohio is home—"

"I'm so excited about our friendship with Alan . . . He's been terrific, hasn't he? If you can do him a favor, we're sure to stay on his good side."

Turner reached for a long thin cigar, lighting it as he continued to listen, smiling as Bunny steered Harry exactly where Turner wanted him to be.

"What can I do for him?" Harriet asked. "He has everything he wants."

"Don't be naive, Harry." Bunny's reprimand was sharp. "Sooner or later, people always need favors. And you can do me one right now by staying away from that woman."

"You have strange fantasies, Bunny. What makes you think she's interested in me?"

Bunny's laugh was a raucous snort. "You men are such fools," she said. "You listen to me Harry Pearl. Stay close to Turner—and far away from Maria Hosada. It's Turner who will get us where we want to be."

Turner heard their room door close. "It's going to work," he said aloud. As he left his study, he did a jaunty two-step toward the door.

The Swans, Pearls, Alan Turner, and Eduardo Gomez, the General's second-in-command, stood at attention in the spacious foyer as General Hosada and Maria made their way down the long staircase of the Palace. A soldier supported the General as he struggled to make sure each foot was placed firmly before he attempted another step. Maria kept a firm grasp on the General's arm, encouraging him as he descended the grand staircase.

81

Maria's gown had been designed to expose as much flesh as possible. Her hair was sculpted and sprayed to look like a crown, delicate jewels sparkling from her golden tresses. Her eyes shone with excitement, her lips glistened a bright ruby red. She was queen of her universe, and with pleasure and satisfaction she took in her domain.

In her excitement over Harry Pearl, she ignored the Swans who seemed only relieved that her attentions had gone elsewhere. As they stood in quiet conversation with Alan Turner, they informed him that one of their grandchildren in New York had fallen seriously ill, and unfortunately they would have to bring their holiday to a close. Turner expressed his regret at the situation, grateful that the illness had not occurred a day earlier. The Swans had served the purpose of luring the Pearls to Los Pagos, and now it was up to him and Maria to take the next step.

Maria had already introduced the Pearls to the General and she was pleased that Papa was enjoying Bunny's charms.

"Permit me the honor of escorting you," the General said to Bunny.

He did his best to lead her into the dining hall, but Bunny had a difficult time keeping the General's heavy body in motion. Slowly they shuffled toward the table.

Trailing behind were Maria and Harry Pearl. Harriet's allergies were reacting to the heavy perfume Maria wore; her eyes began to water. She was having a difficult time breathing.

"Señor Pearl," Maria whispered flirtatiously, "Are you already so excited to be walking next to Maria Hosada?" She giggled as she linked her arm through his. "I will make this a special evening for you, one you will remember."

Harriet smiled at Maria, wiped her eyes and took

another look at the room. A showplace of gilt, marble, crystal, silver, it was also a strange kennel and aviary of sorts. Dogs slept on thick Persian carpets, cats were curled on the large dining room table. Tropical birds flew overhead, their loud cries and bright colors part of the incredible scene.

"The General loves animals so," Maria said. "We have our friends with us always. What about you, Harry? Do you like animals? The cats are especially adorable, don't you think?"

Overhearing the conversation, Bunny said, "Harry doesn't care for felines." Her voice was sharp, her tone possessive. "He has allergies—"

"Which are not affected by rabbits, eh?" Maria asked mischievously, but with an ingratiating smile.

"Rabbits?" the General said. "We have no rabbits, but they might add to our happy family, Maria. Why don't we look into acquiring a pair of spotted hares?"

Bunny turned away from Maria, affecting disapproval of her joke.

Dinner was a spectacle in itself. Dogs awoke and begged for food, cats helped themselves from platters of culinary treats set down for them in the center of the table, and brightly colored birds flew overhead.

After the first course, a chilled, spicy gazpacho, the Swans excused themselves, Mrs. Swan pleading a headache. It was obvious to Bunny that she was not amused by any of the goings on, least of all the ill-concealed flirting of Maria Hosada with Harry Pearl. As she bade the General farewell, a bird bestowed its predictable gift on her head. The General roared with laughter while she reached frantically for a fresh napkin.

"This brings with it the best of luck, Mrs. Swan," he

said, "consider yourself fortunate. Such things would not happen if you were dining in the capitol of your own country."

"You may be assured that you are correct about that," she said. As the couple turned from the table, Bunny heard her add to her husband, "John, we are moving to Palm Springs."

Seated at the far end of the table, Eduardo snapped his fingers to get the waiter's attention. But the waiter was not present at the moment, and so he raised his dull, sleepy eyes and looked at Yarmi, Maria's personal maid. A large, heavy-set woman, she sat comfortably in a wicker chair in the corner of the room fanning herself with a starched, folded napkin. She enjoyed being present at formal dinners and busied herself with little more than enjoying the scene and seeing to any of her mistress's needs.

"Wake up, Yarmi," Eduardo called, "can't you see my wine glass is empty?"

Yarmi smiled vacantly, not hearing Eduardo's request. She nodded pleasantly and reached down to stroke a large black cat which lay curled at her feet.

"Yarmi," he called in a louder voice. "You deaf? Wine! I want wine! Bring it, old lady."

This time Yarmi did hear Eduardo, but so did Maria who stood and glared down the length of the table at the sweating man who had so harshly bellowed his orders.

"You do not speak to Yarmi in that tone, you do not speak to Yarmi at all. She has nothing to do with you . . . and your . . . wine. Here," Maria continued, striding the long table a bottle in each hand. "Here, Eduardo, drink wine . . . all the wine you want." From both hands she poured wine into his glass, red and white mixing in the crystal, touching the brim, overflowing on the tablecloth. "Enough wine, Eduardo?" she asked. "What else do you want?"

84

"Nothing," he said curtly, moving back from the table, the white cloth in front of him soaked crimson.

"Good," Maria sharply replied. She set the bottles in front of his plate and turned to walk away. "Now drink— drink all you want."

Taking her seat next to the General once more, she smiled and reached for his hand. "What a festive dinner party, Papa. We should have them more often."

Following the gazpacho, roasted loins of pork seasoned with lemon juice, garlic and spices were brought to the table. Coucou, a native dish of white cornmeal and fresh okra, was served, then a platter of fiery grilled shrimp and rice. After the dessert of walnut and citrus fruit torte, the men accompanied the General to his study for brandy and cigars. Maria and Bunny were escorted to the sunroom by one of the many servants where Maria sat on a richly brocaded sofa, crossed her legs, and raised her skirt above her knees.

"You got a good looking man," she said with enthusiasm. "Is he a good lover?"

Bunny's body stiffened in defense. "He is a good husband," she said.

"But is he a good lover?" Maria repeated.

"Yes, of course." Primly, Bunny placed her hands in her lap.

Bored, Maria reached for a dish of candies, biting into dark chocolate, cherries, thick creams. She offered the dish to Bunny who declined, preferring the glass of wine that had been placed on the table beside her.

She began talking about Cleveland, wanting to keep the conversation away from Harry, but Maria soon interrupted.

"I don't like to talk about any place but Los Pagos," she said abruptly. "It's because I've never traveled from our shores," she added, softening her tone.

85

"Sorry," Bunny replied. "I do tend to go on about home. Please tell me about your island."

"We're a simple people, Mrs. Pearl, peace-loving, sincere. Poverty is our only problem. We need jobs for our young men and woman. They scratch a living from the land and earn meager wages from the sea as we're too poor to finance a large fishing fleet. Some work in our sugar factories, but we've not kept up with modern technology. Other islands have resorts, casinos, places of excitement for the young that bring money from the tourists. Our island is a lovely setting for a resort, don't you agree?"

"My, yes. With a casino, cruise ships would surely stop here. How exciting! Some of your people might want to open boutiques, there are so many adorable little shops on the other islands."

Maria smiled at Bunny. "You are right and that could present its own problems. Outsiders with capital would own these shops, employ our islanders. Still, they would lead better lives than I knew when I worked long hours in a sugar factory for pennies. That was many years ago, Mrs. Pearl, before I was so honored as to become the General's wife."

"How did you and the General meet?" Bunny asked coyly.

Maria stared at her, then spoke sharply. "I don't like girl talk, Mrs. Pearl. Let's get back to the men." She summoned the servant. "Tell the General we will meet him in the Gold Room. Maria Hosada wants to dance."

Surprised by Maria's abruptness, Bunny stood and followed her hostess from the room. There was a cunning to Maria, Bunny reflected, a shrewd grasp of situations. Turner and the General might think they had control, but

Bunny suspected it was actually Maria Hosada who ruled Los Pagos.

Seated in the study, Harriet wasn't making much progress with Turner and the dozing General.

"The General is at his best in the morning," Turner said in apology. "He is much more alert then."

Just then the servant appeared at the doorway. "Señora Hosada requests your presence in the Gold Room."

The General's head jerked up. "Tell her we're on our way."

As the men entered the room, the small band was already playing. Maria was dancing, alone, softly singing the words of the song over the muted trumpet that carried the melody.

The General was led to a chair where he promptly fell into a deep slumber. Nevertheless, Maria danced over to where he was sitting, picked up his hand and snapped a quick beat with her feet as the band began to play Latin rhythms.

"I always dance with the General first," she said, gyrating to the music. She leaned over, kissed him on the cheek, then danced into the middle of the room.

"Okay Mr. Pearl," she said as she spun around, "let's see how you move to a Latin beat." She danced toward Harriet, took her hand and pulled her out onto the dance floor.

Alan clapped his hands to the rhythm, turned to Bunny and said, "Mrs. Pearl, may I have the pleasure?"

The dancing continued through the evening. Bunny's partners were Turner or Eduardo, whereas Harriet and

Maria, seemingly tireless in their energies, danced on.

Harriet was a light, agile dancer. She persisted in resisting Maria's embraces by executing dance steps that grew more and more intricate, flamboyant, bizarre.

"Ho, ho, my handsome USA, you are one hell of a Fred Astaire," Maria said as she whirled under Harriet's arm.

Harriet was too winded to answer.

Finally, Turner broke in on the couple.

"I have had the workout of a lifetime," Harriet muttered as she returned to Bunny. "Any chance of our leaving?"

"I don't think we'll be missed," Bunny said, looking over at the passionately embracing Maria and Turner. "We can walk back in the moonlight, it's a beautiful night."

Strolling along the water's edge, they discussed the progress they'd made with their plan to entrap Alan Turner, agreeing that so far they'd made none.

"If Maria's acting as the decoy for scooping up the cash," Harriet said, "Turner's hands will be clean. Giving a bundle to Maria isn't going to implicate Turner."

"All we need," Bunny concluded, "is evidence he's involved, we don't have to hand the money over to him."

"But what evidence?" Harriet asked. "And how long do you think I can keep Maria at bay? She's got more on her mind than a few dances."

Bunny laughed. "You'll have to give the staff a taste of your talents at the Christmas party."

Harriet didn't answer. Lost in somber thought, she looked out at the moon reflected in the calm waters of the bay.

Later, lying in bed, wearing only her underwear, Harriet watched Bunny take off her makeup. Then Bunny began to undress, removing her clothes slowly, dropping her garments, one by one, on the floor as she walked about the room. As her last undergarment fell to her side, she turned to face Harriet.

"What do you really think of Maria Hosada?" she asked.

Harriet looked into her eyes for any hints of expression that they were about to begin another conversation for Alan Turner's benefit. She saw none.

"What do you think, Harry Pearl? Does she have a better body than mine? She throws it around enough, that's for sure."

Harriet's eyes scanned the length of Bunny's body. She belonged in a painting by one of the masters. Her body glowed with good health. The wide hips, full breasts, and narrow waist were voluptuously curved.

"Does she, Harry? Answer me," Bunny prodded.

"Of course not," Harriet said haltingly, "you're . . . unbelievable." She meant what she said.

Bunny smiled and walked to the bathroom. When she reappeared, she wore a low-cut peach nightgown.

"I wanted to wear something . . . cool tonight," she said as she turned off the light.

This was the first night they had shared a bed. Harriet moved over to make room, but Bunny snuggled close and wrapped an arm around her, pinching her lightly to let her know that this was for Turner's benefit.

"Sweet dreams, lover," she said. Then she kissed her on the mouth.

Harriet was surprised by the softness of Bunny's lips. She returned the kiss. "Sweet dreams to you, too," she whispered.

Harriet liked being this close to Bunny's soft, enticing warmth. She liked holding her and was disappointed when

Bunny moved away. Through the night, both were restless. There was a tension in the bed that neither dared explore.

Harry tried with all his might to bring reality back into focus, to get the real situation clear in his mind, but Harriet made no attempt to reach out and touch him.

The next morning Harriet awakened surprised to find Bunny's arms wrapped tightly around her. She basked in the good feeling, the tender sensuality. She wanted to caress her, yet didn't want to awaken her. She traced a line across Bunny's forehead, then with the lightest of touches, she grazed her cheeks, her chin, the tip of her nose. When Bunny opened her eyes, Harriet smiled. Then, as if daylight brought with it the harsh light of a new reality, Bunny eased away from Harriet, slipping ever so quietly out of bed. She gathered her clothes and stepped into the bathroom for her morning shower.

Harriet, in an unusually good mood, hummed to herself as she made coffee. She poured glasses of juice and warmed fresh bread. On a tray, she arranged their breakfast and carried it out to the balcony.

Hearing Bunny open the bathroom door, she called, "I'm out here, come have some coffee. It's a beautiful morning."

Bunny stepped onto the balcony blinking back bright sunlight. She took the glass Harriet offered and winced at the taste of cold, tart juice.

"You don't like pineapple, I forgot," Harriet said. "Let me see what else we have."

"Coffee's all I want," Bunny replied.

"Plenty here," Harriet said, smiling at Bunny as she passed a cup.

Bunny pulled her chair into the shade and sat down, turning her back to Harriet.

"What's wrong?" Harriet asked. When Bunny didn't reply, Harriet remembered that Bunny was always quiet in the morning. Why should today be any exception?

A few minutes later, trying to break the mood, Harriet said brightly, "We don't have any plans for this morning, how about a swim? There's a thermos in the kitchen, let's take our coffee down to the beach."

"At nine in the morning?" Bunny asked dourly.

"It doesn't matter what time it is once the sun's up."

"And I guess you're going to swim bare-chested—"

"Come on, Bun, don't be silly. I'll wear jogging shorts and a T-shirt. I can wade . . . take a swim . . . wrap myself in a beach towel when I get out of the water. I'm not about to blow our cover," she said dramatically.

Bunny turned to look at Harriet. She was leaning over the balcony, about to pick a bright red hibiscus blossom. As she stretched, Bunny took in the long, lean lines of her body. "Be careful . . . don't fall," Bunny said, her words a whisper of caution.

Harriet turned and presented the flower. "For you, Madame. To lighten your mood, to brighten your day."

Bunny smiled. "Let's go down to the beach,' she said.

"But wait," Harriet said, taking the flower back from Bunny. She tucked the red blossom above Bunny's ear. "That's what these flowers are for," she said, running her hand through Bunny's thick brown hair.

"I want to change, you go ahead, Harriet," she said softly. "I'll meet you down at the cabana."

Stretched out in a lounge chair, Harriet basked in the

tropical sun. She looked up to see Bunny strolling toward her across the white sand, looking as perfect as the beautiful island morning. When Bunny sat down beside her, Harriet was glad they had the beach to themselves. She knew that there was much about this morning that was different and she knew she couldn't put it all into words herself. She remembered Bunny touching her, her cool fingers tracing a line up and down Harriet's arm, across her shoulders. She sighed, knowing she couldn't put *any* of it into words. It doesn't matter if we talk, Harriet told herself, I just want us to be . . . to be together.

Time passed, and as they sipped their coffee, the tension eased. Harriet opened the tube of sunscreen and squirted a line on each of her legs. "Know what's nice about this role playing?" she asked. "I don't have to shave my legs. After this, I don't know if I'll ever shave them again."

Bunny reached across to rub the sunscreen across Harriet's calves and thighs. "Your legs don't feel like a man's legs at all, your skin's so soft, my darling."

Harriet was speechless.

"How do you like my suit?" Bunny asked. "You usually comment on my clothes. You haven't seen me in a bathing suit before, have you?"

"No," Harriet whispered.

"Too revealing for you?"

"It is a little revealing," Harriet agreed, grateful that Bunny was helping her by lending her words such as those she now spoke.

"For Mrs. Pearl you mean?" Bunny asked.

Harriet turned to Bunny. "Well, I—"

"Or is it that it makes you hot, Harriet?"

Bunny held Harriet's gaze as she waited for an answer.

92

"And the kiss last night—I wanted more than a kiss, Harriet. Didn't you?"

Harriet turned away. She could feel her skin flaming with a heady blush, but she could not answer. She sat up and looked out at the surf.

Bunny reached over and took her hand. Gently she laughed and then continued, "It's all so bizarre, Harriet. You're Maria Hosada's type—that's the key to all this. But if you *were* a man—Driscoll or Fowler or one of the other agents—they never would have sent me because of my reputation. You were safe for me, Harriet, because you *weren't* a man. And now look at what's happening. A psychiatrist would have a field day with me!" She stood, looking down at Harriet, and then sat down beside her. "And what about you, my sweet Harry Pearl? What are you feeling about all this?"

Harriet struggled for the words. It wasn't easy for her to speak. "All these years we've been . . . almost strangers to each other. Yet down here . . . in these outfits I wear . . . look what's happened."

"What *has* happened? And is it just because of your . . . outfits?" Bunny asked gently.

"No, of course not. Who would have known we'd have so much in common . . . " Her words faded away, then she tried again. "I have wonderful feelings about you. As a person . . . "

"I have wonderful feelings about you, too," Bunny said, "but it's more than just as a person . . . as a friend. Do you know what I'm saying, Harriet? Don't turn away. Look at me. I want to see the expression in your eyes."

"I don't know what to say, Bunny. I can't explain what I feel."

The expression in Harriet's eyes, however, told Bunny

all she needed to know.

Bunny reached for a large towel and covered the two of them as they lay in the beach chair.

"You don't want to burn your skin, Harriet, you're having enough trouble with that makeup in this heat."

Harriet sighed and then, forgetting who she was supposed to be, but thinking later that it was certainly something Harry Pearl might have done, she wrapped her arms around Bunny and held her tenderly. They lay together for the longest time. It was Bunny who broke the spell.

"Harry Pearl, it's time to go back to work."

VI

Reclining on an ornate wicker lounge, the General was shaded by leafy palms rippling in the cool morning breezes. A pet toucan preened its bright plumage as he offered it slivers of pineapple from a silver tray. The fresh fruit glistened in the bright sunlight but the bird was not tempted.

"How vain you are, old friend," Hosada said. "This fruit was brought especially for you. Groom your fine feathers after breakfast."

As if in reply, the bird opened its large beak and squawked shrilly. In response, the General laughed and began eating the pineapple himself, juice running down his hands onto the sleeves of his satin dressing gown. He reached for a linen napkin and wiped his fingers. As he enjoyed the morning air, he was pleased that the events Alan Turner had been so anxious to put into motion were about to begin.

Though he felt confident that they would soon enjoy success, the General still had many questions. That Turner asked for so little for himself was suspicious. A finder's fee only, Turner had claimed. Twenty thousand dollars, sufficient to pay off pressing debts.

"I may still stand a chance of an ambassadorship, General. I can't afford a noticeable amount of money suddenly in my bank account, or to have my name connected to any projects that might raise questions in the State Department," he'd said. "The years ahead are important to my career."

The General had considered Turner's position carefully. He knew his own destiny was limited by time; his age made it all the more important to assure his peaceful island of economic security.

My people have never enjoyed prosperity, he reflected, and they deserve this. My Maria deserves it. She wants so much . . . and all of it for good purposes. I want to see the completion of the hospital she so badly desires.

This is where you have been helpful to me, Turner, he ruminated. The casino will assure us of the sums we need while a secure military police will discourage interference from foreigners. I don't want outsiders meddling, I don't want them gaining a foothold to any door except that of the casino itself. There can be no threat to our government, to our future—all must be secure for Maria and Eduardo.

Hearing footsteps, he turned to see Alan Turner walking toward him.

"You are late," Hosada said. "I like to have the day's business completed before the sun climbs over the crest of Mount Alba."

96

"I know, General, but our conversation will be brief. The time is right to invite Harry Pearl to join us as our major investor."

"Is it, Turner?" he asked skeptically. "You feel our charming friend is in the mood to present me with millions of American dollars?"

"Yes, I know he can be persuaded. Besides, his wife's easy game and he'll do as she says."

"I don't trust a man like that."

Turner laughed. "You want the money, don't you? Since our first discussions, I've considered many possibilities. None of them have been right. He's our man."

"What makes you so sure? And what are you after, Mr. Turner, besides this . . . finder's fee? You want my wife, don't you?"

"Any man would want your wife, General," Turner said quickly. "But I respect honor, I can assure you."

The General persisted. "I think you're up to something else . . . I want to know what that is. You are a diplomat who understands the complex issues of world politics. I am a simple peasant who knows only the island of his birth and I believe that much of life can be seen as either black or white. You I see as grey and that worries me. To get the money I need, I must overlook this but don't think for a moment that I trust you. Knowing this, do you still want to proceed with this plan of yours?"

"Of course. It will work, I know it. Have I not arranged your purchase of guns and munitions—as I promised—to strengthen your military police? You will soon learn that I am trustworthy in all ways, General."

With the pet toucan now on his arm, the General fed it the last sliver of fruit. "You were almost too late, my handsome fellow. I would have finished the pineapple myself."

You will have your way, Turner ... about this, he decided, but I do not believe you are honorable. Your finder's fee is a ploy. I'm not sure what else you desire, but I will not permit you to join forces with Maria to destroy Eduardo. I won't have Eduardo threatened by your presence on Los Pagos any longer than necessary. After the funds have been committed for the casino, I will see that you will go elsewhere, whether it be to an ambassadorship or another distant consulate, I do not care.

He looked up at Turner, clapped his hands and said, "Then bring it about quickly."

Shortly after arriving at the General's palace that day for a buffet luncheon, the Pearls were separated. The Hosadas had planned that the General would present his proposal to Harry while Maria, accompanied by Turner, persuaded Bunny to accept the glamorous ceremonial position of Los Pagos' official hostess at the casino.

"As exciting as the casino will be, I cannot abandon my duties to my people ... to the church ... to our orphanage. Yes, even here on Los Pagos there are babies abandoned ... and I must care for them. You, Bunny Pearl, if you desire it, will greet and extend the hospitality of Los Pagos to those wealthy and exciting travelers who will come to us from far, far away. Does this appeal to you?"

Bunny's reaction was convincingly enthusiastic. "Yes, of course, but I've had no experience—"

"As with many other things in life, you will learn as you go. And you have a great gift for charm," Maria said admiringly. "Who would be better? I choose you. Understand?"

Bunny expected that Turner would support Maria, but he sat, listened, and said nothing. When Maria excused

98

herself to attend to the General, Bunny asked him what he thought of the idea.

"I'm in no position to encourage you but it does seem to be a rare opportunity. Still, it is only a dream. The General has found no one willing to make that kind of financial commitment to Los Pagos."

"Why? It seems to be such an exciting idea."

"Of course, but this is the land of banana republics, isn't it? Problems could arise at any time."

"You mean like Cuba? A resort haven shut down because of politics?"

Turner laughed, then looked at her as if she were a child. "No, no, Bunny, Los Pagos has no armed forces worth mentioning."

His voice cool with disdain, he continued, "The natives here are basically lazy, therefore they are helpless, poor. Nothing motivates them—they work only when necessary and mañana is the only day they know."

"What do you mean then?"

"There are risks in any business proposition. Has your husband kept you so safely in the dark?"

Bunny didn't attempt to answer the question. It was apparent to her that Turner would have no active part in this deal other than extending a vague enticement to what he perceived as a social climbing woman.

"The General and Mr. Pearl are deep in conversation," Maria said, coming back into the room. "I'd like to show Bunny some of the preliminary renderings, Alan. Would you excuse us for a few moments?"

"Of course." He walked toward the door. "You two have much to discuss. As for me, I have letters that need to be answered. I'll see you in a bit."

"Come," Maria said to Bunny, "let me show you what we have in mind."

As they walked into a large, spacious office, Bunny was surprised to see work being done at a drafting table.

"This is Mr. Montoya, our consultant," Maria said. "He brings his engineering and architectural skills all the way from Caracas. What do we have to show Mrs. Pearl, Carlos?"

"What would she like to see?" Montoya asked, rising to shake Bunny's hand. "I have topographic studies, blueprints, what's your interest?"

"I don't know," Bunny replied. "Where should we begin?"

"Show her the renderings for the entire projected development. The casino is only one part of it, Bunny. We'll have restaurants, guest houses, a beach club . . . It's all so exciting! The concept is sure to interest you and your husband."

As the large drawings were unrolled and laid out on the desk, Maria smiled broadly and said, "It's magnificent, Carlos. Each time I look at the sketches, I grow more enthusiastic."

"Good," he replied. "And what of the General? Has he seen these new renderings?"

"No, of course not," Maria said quickly, "but I've told him in detail about them. What we agree upon, he will accept."

"Earlier he expressed some concern about the height of the hotel—"

"Carlos," my husband is old, his mind wanders these days. What is important to him one day is only a memory, if that, the next. His signature will be needed to begin construction, but it is my approval which must be met first," she said with authority. "Now explain the layouts to Mrs. Pearl."

That there was tension between Maria and the Venezuelan engineer was obvious to Bunny. Maria was unyielding in her control of the plans for the resort. It was clear that Maria was the moving force on the island, the old man little more than a colorful figurehead. More than once she'd observed Maria making quick, efficient decisions concerning routine business matters; no one had access to General Hosada before Maria knew exactly what each visitor desired. Bunny turned her attention to the drawings and listened to the explanation of all that would come to be.

General Hosada spoke abruptly, and to the point. "I understand you are a wealthy man, Mr. Pearl, correct?"

Harriet's expression was as direct as her answer. "Yes General, I am. I've been most fortunate in my investments."

"Good. I believe in what you Americans call industriousness. Apparently, your financial future is secure. Now what do you want to do with the rest of your life? You are young, what are your dreams?" With effort the General shifted his bulk in the massive leather chair which dominated his study.

Harriet smiled. "Only to spend more of my time with my wife. She is my dream."

The General reached over to his desk where he opened a silver humidor embossed with his initials. He selected two cigars and offered one to Harriet. "No more conquests? No other women? No other fortunes?"

"I have all that I need, General, I have no burning desires." Harriet accepted the cigar. "Thank you, General. I'm in the mood to enjoy a smoke."

He nodded and took a bronze lighter from the pocket of his khaki bush jacket. "And what of the beautiful Mrs. Pearl? What does she want from life?"

"To spend more time with me, naturally." Harriet

examined the cigar, took in the rich odor of the tightly rolled leaves of tobacco, bit off the tip and accepted the General's light. She inhaled deeply, stretched out her legs and crossed her feet. "And though I don't fully understand her reasons," Harriet continued, "my wife wants to move in more sophisticated social circles than we have up to now."

"Ah, then I *can* be of help to you. You and your wife are charming, very likable ... I want to make myself available to you and ... Bunny, yes?"

"Thank you, General Hosada." Harriet blew a perfect smoke ring, then another. For a second, they came together in a filmy figure eight, then drifted off.

"De nada ... it is nothing, as we say here. We both love our wives, we work hard to please them, to satisfy them. Your wife needs society, my wife needs the feeling of satisfaction that comes from helping others. She is devoted to our people. Totally."

"And?" Harriet asked, waiting for the General to unfold his plan.

"And I now offer you the opportunity to provide your wife with the social circle she so desires. It is my wish to establish a casino and resort hotel which will bring sleepy Los Pagos into the twentieth century. We will need someone to act as our country's representative, but Maria will not relinquish her work with our people. This person will be at the center of all that is happening. This person could—will, if you so desire it—be your wife. It is an important function, Harry Pearl." The General, feeling tired from the conversation but knowing he must continue, poured a glass of ice cold water from a carafe on the small table next to his chair. He drank deeply, smacking his lips as he emptied the glass, a small river of water running through his hoary beard.

"Why are you being so generous to us? We are strangers to you—"

Feeling refreshed from the icy water, the General spoke in a deep, hearty voice. "Destined to be friends, and more than that. Partners. I will provide your wife with what she wants and you, Harry, will provide me with what I want."

"Which is?"

"Financial backing. But it must come soon. We've chosen the land, a beautiful spot. I can show it to you tomorrow, if you like. The engineers have finished the boring tests necessary to assure that the site is adequate to support high-rise buildings. I'd like you to meet with them. You're intelligent ... I'm sure you'll have questions to ask, and your own people to check with, to confirm the desirability of this investment. You will reap great rewards, but your commitment needn't be only financial. I want you and your wife to be as active as you wish in the resort." The General smiled as he waited for Harry's response. But his hand shook as he poured another glass of water and he felt very tired.

"We know nothing about hotel and resort management," Harriet replied with cool objectivity. "We can offer you nothing in the way of experience."

"You can finance me, Mr. Pearl. I want this project to move ahead. I've been looking for a man like you for a long time ... I feel I can trust you, and I trust my instincts. You're the partner I want. With Turner's connections we'll attract the clientele we need. Bunny will charm them into returning, and you will quickly realize substantial profits."

"Turner is a diplomat on leave, General, not a specialist in tourism. Or is he in on this deal?"

"Of course not. But he knows the kind of people we want at an exclusive resort. Inviting them here presents no conflict of interest for him, it is simply extending the hospitality of the island to all who care to partake. Do you not agree?" Overcome by fatigue, the General knew he did not have the strength to carry on the conversation much longer.

Harriet didn't answer. It was clear, however, that Turner was protected by the General, probably by Maria as well.

"Don't be hasty, Mr. Pearl." The General rose unsteadily to his feet. "Take the time you need to make your decision. If you wish, we'll meet with the engineers after we tour the site. For now, we have had enough business." He clapped his hands and a white-jacketed servant rushed in to assist him. "It is time to join the others," he said as he was helped from the room.

Harriet and Bunny strolled hand in hand along the beach. Eagerly, they told each other of all that had transpired that day. Harriet brought Bunny up to date on the latest encounter with Turner.

"He was on his way to the gym, I told him how the General had approached me with this idea of his for a casino. He didn't discourage me, he didn't encourage me ... So unless there's a slipup somewhere his hands are going to be clean."

"Didn't he say *anything?*"

"Sure—he told me he wanted us to enjoy ourselves. He wants me to join him in a drive to the mountains tonight to see one of the local cockfights."

"Without me?" Bunny asked.

"It's not a sport the ladies indulge in. Anyway," Harriet said lightly, "wouldn't you rather I spend a night out with Turner than Maria?"

104

"I suppose so," Bunny said, deeply disappointed that they wouldn't be together that evening. "But what else did he say?"

"Only that the General's had this idea for a long time. From what you say, it's my guess the idea originated with Maria." Harriet turned to Bunny and squeezed her hand. "Look, we know Turner's involved in this but how are we going to expose him?"

"Maria will help us there," Bunny said. "Sooner or later she's bound to implicate him."

"Can't you get any information from her? The two of you spend enough time together."

Bunny looked up at Harriet and laughed. "Oh no, handsome, she has eyes only for you. She's with me only out of necessity."

"Then how do we get her to open up?"

"Three guesses," Bunny said.

"Oh, no," Harriet groaned.

"Oh, yes."

"But how?"

"You'll find a way. Don't forget all the information we have on her past romances."

"I'd rather not think about it."

"Do you really mean that?" Bunny asked, looking into Harriet's eyes.

"Yes," Harriet said, embracing Bunny, "oh, yes."

Bunny held Harriet close. "What now?" she asked.

"I wish I knew," Harriet replied.

As the sun's bright rays poured over the western tip of the island, Maria decided it was an ideal time to invite the Pearls for a grand tour. The early hours of evening were cool, the light cast the island in a lovely golden glow.

Later, the men would part company from the group and make their journey by jeep to the championship cockfight.

Maria insisted that Bunny sit next to Turner who would drive her white Cadillac. She climbed into the back seat pulling Harriet in after her.

"Come on, handsome, keep me company for at least a little while," she said as she smoothed her full skirt and tucked it under her thighs. "Alan," she called, "try to miss the potholes. It's hell getting parts from the States."

Her mood was jubilant as she directed Turner to maneuver the sharpest of the hairpin curves on the rutted dusty road. Within minutes, the white car was covered with dust.

"Here, Harry," she said, passing him a handful of hard candies which she took from a garnet ceramic jar, "now you'll get to see our beautiful children."

The car approached a cluster of *ajoupa* houses, the framework woven from young saplings, the exterior plastered with clay. Thatched roofs were made of bound bundles of thick grasses; low-hanging eaves offered protection from sun or rain. Not only children but men and women of the small village approached the car greeting Maria with waves and salutations of love. Harriet tossed candies to the excited children as Maria watched.

"You're enjoying your task so," Maria said as she casually placed her hand on white linen trousers. "Such beautiful children, aren't they?"

"They're wonderful," Harriet said. She turned to Maria and smiled, stretching her left arm across the top of the back seat, her fingers lightly caressing Maria's bare shoulders.

"That's the way of our island, USA," she responded softly as she moved closer to Harriet. "I take it you approve."

How handsome he is, Maria thought, looking at the

106

blond hair ruffled by the wind. She ran her hand down the sleeve of a crisp blue shirt, her fingers resting on the white trousers once more. "It's sweet that you give to Maria's babies," she said, "but of course our people need much, much more than sweets . . . than candies."

"I know," Harriet said taking Maria's hand and holding it in her own. As Bunny turned in her seat, they quickly moved apart.

"You have a loving and generous husband, Bunny. He's having such fun passing treats to our children."

"Shall we get out and stroll a bit?" Turner asked.

"I'd like that," Harriet said. "How about you, Bun?"

"Of course," Bunny said cheerfully.

Turner parked the car in the tiny village square. As they stepped out onto the dirt road, Bunny caught her breath. "Harry, look," she said with delight.

Maria laughed at the Pearls' astonishment as a family of peacocks meandered across the square. "Haven't you seen these birds before?" she asked.

"Only in cages," Harriet replied, "and none were as beautiful as these."

As the birds disappeared into the brush, Maria said, "Come, I want my friends to meet you. Perhaps they will be as astonished by you as you were by the birds. They've not met many Americans."

Maria linked her arm through Harriet's as Alan and Bunny walked ahead. Harriet asked, "How many live in this village?"

"Over a thousand," Maria replied. "This is a typical village of the island."

Harriet looked at the small cluster of homes, thinking that they would house no more than sixty people. "Then this square is home for only a few dozen families."

"Yes, most live back from the main road. People reach

107

their homes by walking the footpaths. Here in the square we have the shopkeepers. Isn't it similar in your country?"

"Yes," Harriet replied, thinking of vast shopping centers that had grown to be the hub of sprawling suburban landscapes.

"Alan," Maria called, "I want to visit Margarita while we're here." She smiled at Harriet and said, "She is a very special friend. You and your wife will admire her wares."

At the edge of the village, they stopped in front of a tiny yellow house. Maria separated from the party and stepped forward to tap lightly on the rickety door. "Are you sleeping, Margarita? Don't let me disturb you if you are."

The door opened and an ancient, tiny woman stood before them, her ebony skin glistening in the sunlight that fell across her doorway.

"I knew you would come today," she said reaching out for Maria's hand. Then she looked up through the bright sunlight to the others standing behind Maria. Her smile broadened. "You have brought me a fair one," she said, looking at Harriet. "I have not seen such a one in many, many years."

"Ah," Maria said, turning to Harriet in admiration, "this is USA."

"USA," the aged woman echoed.

"Mr. Harry Pearl, Mrs. Bunny Pearl and Consul Turner. He has been with me before, of course."

"I remember."

"May we step inside?" Maria asked. "I would like to show my friends some of your work."

"Of course ... I have just completed the gift I promised you."

As she stepped back to allow the others to enter her hut, Bunny left Alan and stood next to Harriet, squeezing her hand. Slowly their eyes adjusted to the darkness and then they saw a vast collection of wood carvings.

"Margarita is our finest artist," Maria said.

"I only try," she said modestly. "See what I have made you, does it please you?" From the dirt floor, she lifted a large covered dish stained a deep red. A pattern of leaves and birds had been cut into the wood, an intricate design carved around the pedestal base.

Maria took the dish and turned it slowly, admiring its artistry. "It is beautiful, Margarita. It will grace our home . . . a treasure."

With a slight nod of her head and upper torso, Margarita bowed. "You are pleased," she said smiling. "Now I will ask you and your friends to sit. Have you time to visit?"

"Yes, yes . . . of course," Maria said, gesturing for all to sit on the large cushions placed against the walls of the hut.

When they left a short while later, Bunny and Harriet had purchased their own favorites from the many works Margarita had shown them, Bunny selecting a seated woman playing a primitive flute, Harriet choosing an urn carved in the same intricate fashion as the bowl which had been made for Maria.

"We have many talents on our island," Maria said, "but none surpass Margarita's."

Though the evening sun was still a burning orange disk on the horizon, a pale moon and evening stars now glimmered against the azure sky. As they walked back to their car, a tall man stepped toward them.

"Señora Hosada," he said in a soft voice, "have you a moment?"

"Alfredo," she replied, "yes. You want news of the sugar contracts, I know. How is work proceeding?"

"Within ten days the current contracts will be filled. Have others arrived?"

109

Maria shook her head. "No, I was hoping that we would move ahead with production, but until the contracts arrive, it doesn't seem wise—"

"And so?" he asked with concern.

"And so we must close down the factories once more." Her voice was flat in resignation. She stopped and looked down at Alfredo. "And you, my general manager, must tell the workers."

"When will we hear, Señora? I must offer them something."

"Tell them Maria Hosada herself will contact the major buyers. I will find a market for our sugar—at a decent price."

"I will give them your message," he said, and bowed.

Maria watched Alfredo walk down one of the footpaths, then disappear into the darkness of thick foliage. She walked back to the car alone while Turner accompanied Bunny and Harriet.

As they began the return trip, Maria said softly, "Not all of Los Pagos is paradise, but I wanted to show you some of the best, USA."

Then Maria was lost in thought. Harriet reflected on the exchange with Alfredo; she could feel Maria's urgency for the casino, for something—anything—that would provide economic security and growth for the people of her island nation.

Some distance from the village, Turner looked in the rear view mirror at Harriet. "You still in the mood for some local excitement?"

"Definitely," Harriet replied.

"You're in luck then, because we're going to Victory Peak tonight. If we want to see the tournament from the beginning, we should be on our way as soon as we return to the Palace with the ladies."

110

"I'm ready," Harriet replied in as hearty a tone as she could muster.

"Good. It'll go on into the wee hours, though. Might be early morning before we're back, better kiss your wife goodnight, Harry. And don't you worry, Bunny, your husband's in safe hands."

"I am sure he is," she said sweetly, "when he is with you."

The two couples chatted casually for the remainder of the drive back to the Palace. After the car was parked and goodbyes were being said, Bunny was aware of Maria's response to the parting kiss between herself and Harriet. So with everything else she's got on her mind, Bunny thought, she still has her eye on Harry.

"May we take this jeep for the mountain road?" Turner asked Maria.

"Of course," she replied, "I will spend a quiet evening with the General."

"Don't be upset by your converstation with Alfredo," Turner said in a confidential tone, "your fortunes will soon be much brighter."

"I hope so," she said wearily. "The people are deserving of more."

"And they will have it," Turner said with conviction.

Bunny waved goodbye as Harriet and Turner drove off in the jeep. "I always thought cockfights were so violent," she said to Maria. "I'm certainly glad we're not going along."

"It's only for the men," Maria replied. Then she took Bunny's hand and said, "I'm very tired from our outing, Bunny. I hope you don't mind if I join the General now. I will have dinner brought to your cottage, if you don't find it rude of me."

"No," Bunny assured her. "I want to think about our

lovely visit to the village and I'd like to turn in early myself."

Maria smiled at her and Bunny sensed a sadness behind her expression which she doubted had anything to do with the flirtation that was going on with Harry. More likely, Bunny thought, she was concerned about the lack of future sugar contracts.

Darkness fell quickly as Turner drove the jeep into the high hills. They made their way up the mountain road, the incessant murmuring sounds from surrounding trees and shrubs filling the moist tropical air.

Turner shifted to first gear and flicked on the fog lights. "It's hell to see on this road at night. Ever been to a cockfight before?"

"Never," Harriet replied after clearing her throat, "I thought they were illegal."

Turner laughed. "They are in most of the civilized world, but Los Pagos retains several quaint customs from the past. I presume you want to take in as many different aspects of island life as time allows," he continued, "and although our visit with Margarita no doubt had a certain charm to it, this is a night for us men to be together. Great gamblers, these islanders, the stakes will be high. It's the last night of the Tournament Royale."

"Which is?"

"The final event culminating twelve round robin matches, pitting, I dare say, some of the meanest cocks in the western hemisphere. I've placed my money on Hernando and I suggest you wager a modest bet yourself."

"I'll do that," Harriet said, sinking back into the leather seat, wondering how Bunny was spending the evening.

"Look ahead, Harry," Turner said, his voice rising with

excitement, "see the fires blazing on Victory Peak? That's our destination."

Harriet reached for a cigar and lighter. She lit up and inhaled. "Looks like it's going to be quite a night, Alan."

"View it as an educational experience," Turner said satirically.

A few minutes later, Turner parked the jeep in the small clearing near the mountain peak. There were no other vehicles; the other men had climbed the steep hill on foot. Deep voices, loud, boisterous, drowned out the murmurous insects.

"The fun's already begun," Turner said. "Let's go see what's happening."

Turner led Harriet to the circular cockpit which was surrounded by white-shirted men. Their grinning faces were shining in the light from tall blazing torches. Turner and his guest were treated with deference as the natives moved back to allow the two to approach the thin wire net circling the ring. Trainers, standing at opposite sides of the ring, held large, struggling birds in their arms.

"Take a look at their spurs—they're steel—used to be silver, but silver's too soft."

Harriet, who had never liked even the sight of blood, clutched her stomach and concentrated on thoughts of Bunny back in their cottage.

Turner slapped Harriet on the back. "Come on, pal, let's place that bet and get you a drink."

"Sure," Harriet replied, relieved to be able to move away from ringside.

Bets placed and drinks in hand, they returned to the cockpit. Turner didn't want to miss any of the events.

"These birds come from pedigreed lines going back to the beginning of the last century," Turner informed his guest. "They're the true royalists of this island. They're

113

raised on raw beef and hard-boiled eggs, rubbed down with ammonia and alcohol to toughen their skins, groomed weekly, feathers and combs cut back as much as possible so they don't make easy targets for their opponents, then trained for several weeks before their first match."

Harriet watched the trainers whispering words of encouragement to their birds, then a whistle was blown, a referee climbed into the pit, surveyed the terrain, stepped out to a small platform that overlooked the ring, raised his right arm and brought it down swiftly, and the cocks were released, shouts from the crowd encouraging the swift, stalking birds.

"Hernando's the smaller of the two," Turner said, "but he's as fast and as mean as they come. Pancho is his opponent." Turner finished his drink, threw the cup on the ground, and began clapping as he shouted, "Her-nan-do! Her-nan-do!"

The birds seemed to respond to the excited men. They circled the ring for several seconds, then Pancho flew at Hernando, his right spur seeming to be aimed at the other bird's eye. Hernando was too swift for him; he moved back, then launched his own attack. Harriet closed her eyes, feeling nothing but revulsion as the rousing cries from the crowd encouraged this fight to the death. She stepped back from the ring, stood in darkness and looked at the tongues of flame blazing from the torches as she tried to block out the cries of the men and the fighting cocks.

And then it was apparently over. Hernando was lifted from the ring by his trainer; he was victorious. Pancho's battered body was lifted on the end of a shovel and tossed into the darkness where the barking dogs no doubt devoured the defeated bird.

Harriet just wanted to go home, but Turner was intent on staying for the final round robin tournament. Six matches followed, the pitch and fever of the night increasing, a crescendo of violence erupting on the mountain top.

She succeeded in numbing herself to much of the gory spectacle by drinking deeply from the bottles of rum that were passed from man to man. Finally, Harriet saw the first morning star in the distant sky. How long can this go on, she asked herself.

And then a thin band of crimson crossed the sky as Hernando was thrown back into the ring to take on his final opponent, a feisty cock named Ramon. Harriet turned and walked away.

It was broad daylight when Turner found Harriet sitting in the jeep. "Whatdya think, Harry, wasn't this all I told you it would be?" His eyes glistened with excitement though his voice was thick with emotion and his words were slurred.

Harriet had no reply, but after she took a good look at the consul, she climbed down from the jeep, took the key from his hand, and helped him into the passenger's seat. "Let's go home," she said tiredly.

As she drove down the mountain road, she realized she'd learned very little. The only information Turner had offered, and that was very early in the evening, was that the General had experienced difficulties finding financial backers because of his dictatorship of the island. Turner felt that this could work in Harry Pearl's favor, though. Hosada would have to give him a bigger slice of the pie . . . a larger share in the profits. Turner had no doubt that those profits would be considerable.

Even though the news was scant, Harriet wanted to tell

Bunny about it before she exhaustedly fell asleep. Bunny was still sleeping when Harriet finally walked back into their bedroom, and so peacefully that Harriet decided against waking her. Without bothering to undress, she lay down on the bed beside her.

VII

The next day Maria was in high spirits. She kept placing her hands on the tall, blond American, Mr. USA. Bunny was Harriet's sole protector; as long as they were together, she was safe. But Harriet knew it was only a matter of time before Maria found a way to separate them.

In the face of Maria's covert flirtatiousness, Bunny became more possessive, more aggressive. Harriet found herself sexually aroused by Bunny's attentions. At these most crucial moments of their assignment, the promise of success for the job was fading and her own desire for Bunny was growing.

Before dinner that evening, in the Hosadas' bedroom, the General said to Maria, "These two love birds of Turner's aren't going to work out. Pearl's hedging about something. My instincts tell me he's not a gambler. He's a cautious fellow, not one to take risks with his investments. Let's not waste any more time on them."

Maria took the General's hand, raised it to her lips and kissed it. "It *will* work, Papa."

The General chuckled. "Perhaps you haven't been sufficiently charming. I've never known you to fail with any man."

She smiled. "I'll have to try a bit harder, Papa."

He doesn't know how much I want this Harry Pearl . . . if only for a night.

Remembering Harry's fingers grazing her shoulders the day before, the fond expression in his eyes, the sweetness of his smile, she thought, *I'm sure he's attracted to me. If I could just get him away from his wife . . .*

The General reflected on Maria's conviction. *If she is sure the Pearls will invest the money,* he decided, *I must trust her.*

As the sun dipped low in the heavens, Yarmi assisted Maria with her preparations for the evening's activities. Her thick peasant hands gently massaged rich cream into Maria's skin.

"Your complexion is so beautiful, my mistress, not a single blemish. Why do you prepare your skin to wear such heavy makeup? It hides your gentleness. Why disguise yourself so?" Yarmi's words were spoken slowly in her mellow, low-pitched voice.

Maria opened her eyes and smiled into the beloved old face. Etched into the tanned skin seemed to be the memories of all that Yarmi had known and seen; it was a face that conveyed the strength of endurance.

"Ah, my faithful one," Maria answered, "you are the

118

reader of my mind. What don't you know? What tricks can I get away with with you? Thank God your son, my confessor, only hears my daily sins. Imagine if he could read my mind—"

"You are a good Catholic," Yarmi answered in staunch tones, "a follower of the Church. You do not sin for not telling of your desires and dreams. I have my way of knowing those, I think ... and my son has his way of knowing the peace you seek in your soul. We have different talents, my son and I ... though his are by far the greatest."

"He cannot see into the future as you can," Maria replied as she reached for a cloth to wipe the thick cold cream from her face.

Yarmi is right, Maria thought, looking at her reflection in the mirror. Without the sharp lines she drew on it to dramatize her expression, the face was soft and sweet.

"This is my warrior's face," Maria said, beginning to apply her base makeup. "It tricks men ... though perhaps not my husband."

Yarmi laughed. "Your warrior's face? And what of your dyed blonde hair? Does that also help you to do battle?"

"You do not like my golden mane?" She shook her head vigorously and fluffed the thick hair about her shoulders. "It is a symbol to my people," she said emphatically. "It gives me strength, Yarmi for the time when I will come to represent the lioness of democracy on this island."

"Then you must make General Hosada understand that after his passing you should govern Los Pagos."

Maria sighed. "I have tried and tried, Yarmi. Perhaps you will have to help me persuade him." She waved her eyebrow pencil in the air as if it were a miniature baton. "What do you think of our American guests, the Pearls?"

"I have many feelings," Yarmi replied mysteriously, bringing Maria's gown to the front of her dressing room.

"Yes?" Maria prompted.

"My feelings are not good," Yarmi admitted as she turned to Maria, a troubled expression on her face.

"What is wrong?" Maria asked.

"I feel much . . . "

"Tell me. Do not hide your feelings from me."

"You will not like what I say. This Mr. Pearl . . . his wife as well . . . They are not to be trusted. They are frauds."

"That can't be," Maria said sharply. "Alan had a thorough check done on them."

"He is an impostor," Yarmi replied. "He is bait."

Maria laughed. "Sweet bait, Yarmi. And remember, you're not always right about your feelings."

"You asked me mistress, you told me not to hide my thoughts."

"I know, I know," Maria answered, taking Yarmi's large hand in her own. "What else do you sense about Mr. and Mrs. Pearl?"

"She will never let him go," Yarmi said bluntly.

"That may be so, but it needn't concern us."

"What is most important," Yarmi continued, "is that I felt the presence of evil in the room as you all sat down to dinner. There was a searching for power that will not be attained."

"I'm sure the table *was* surrounded by ambition," Maria replied, "some good, I hope. I don't know enough about the Pearls yet, but I do know Alan and the General. The only evil force in the room—the only one who would destroy—was Eduardo. But he cannot put deeds into motion without the General's consent."

Yarmi's expression became animated. She spoke excitedly. "You felt what I did, mistress. You talked just now of destruction, of destroying—"

"I never meant that." Maria frowned as she stood in front of her dressing table.

Yarmi knelt before her and grasped her hands. "Let us say our prayers, mistress. Maria Hosada must have God on her side."

At the dinner table, the General was telling Bunny stories of his rise to glory. Thinking she had a few moments to herself, Harriet stepped out onto the terrace. She bit off the tip of one of the General's fine Cuban cigars and flicked it into the bushes. She lit the cigar, inhaled and sighed with contentment. But the heavy musk of Maria's perfume made her realize that the contentment was to be short-lived.

Maria, coming up behind her, took the cigar from Harriet's hand and threw it over the terrace. "Do you want to ruin your beautiful lungs?" she asked. Impulsively, she wrapped her arms around Harriet's waist. She leaned against Harriet's back, then her hands caressed Harriet's shoulders. "You've wanted this as much as I, haven't you?" Maria whispered.

As Harriet broke away and turned to face her, Maria suddenly kissed her on the lips.

"My wife—your General—what are you doing?"

"Ah, Harry Pearl," Maria said, running her hands up and down the length of Harriet's thin body, "my beloved General understands my needs. And as for your charming wife, she can have whatever she wants here on Los Pagos."

"But she wants me!"

"How naive you are. She wants social power. I will see that she gets it."

121

Struggling to free herself from Maria, Harriet tried another tactic. "Turner's involved in these plans for a resort, isn't he? How? Are you all partners in the deal? I want to know what you're up to."

Maria laughed and stepped back. "Naive—but not stupid, Harry Pearl. I promise you we'll discuss Turner when the time is right."

"I won't give up a cent until I know exactly who the other investors are in this project and who's behind it. I'm making that a condition beginning right now, before negotiations proceed any further."

Now that there was a condition Maria could meet, she felt confident of her conquest. "That's more than fair," she said, looking him directly in the eyes. "We'll discuss all of this again." Then she turned to walk away saying, "It's time to put the General to bed and tell him the good news. Sweet dreams, USA."

Harriet smoothed her clothing and walked back inside. Bunny wasn't at the table, she was nowhere in the room. Harriet walked back to their quarters wondering why Bunny had left, wondering if she had witnessed the scene with Maria. But it was all part of the assignment . . .

Bunny undressed, removed her makeup, and anxiously awaited Harriet's return. How could she be this jealous of Maria? In frustration, in rage, she paced the room, then removed the bugging devices.

Later, as she heard Harriet come in, she walked to the top of the stairs. "Have a good time?" she asked icily.

"I was talking to Maria," Harriet explained.

"It must have been *some* conversation. That's her lipstick on your face, isn't it?"

"Bunny, I got her to agree—I think—to give me the

information we need on Turner. She as much as admitted to me that Turner is involved, she just didn't say how. But when we give the money to—"

Bunny interrupted, "What did she actually tell you? Anything?" As Harriet began walking up the steps toward her, she said, "Take a shower. I don't want to smell that perfume factory all night long."

A few minutes later, dressed in her underwear, Harriet walked back into the bedroom and sat down on the edge of their bed. She felt miserable and confused.

"I'm trying to do my job, Bunny, that's all," Harriet began. "Can I help it if she's fallen for me?"

At the serious expression on Harriet's face, Bunny, seated on the sofa, began to laugh. "Don't take it to heart so. Come on over here, you big lug."

She opened her arms wide but Harriet only stared at her. "What's the matter?" Bunny coaxed. "Can't I compete with the beautiful Maria?"

"What are you? Drunk?" Harriet said impatiently.

"Drunk on you maybe ... Did you ever think this would happen?" She sat down beside Harriet. "I'm not kidding, don't think this is a joke." She brushed Harriet's hair back from her forehead, embraced her tenderly and whispered, "I think I know how you feel about me. I want us to make love."

Harriet sighed.

"Is that all you're going to do?" Bunny asked.

When Harriet didn't respond, Bunny stood up. "It's too hot for a nightgown," she said, letting the filmy silken gown fall from her shoulders, over her body and down to the floor.

"It's so close tonight ... so humid ... you must be sticky in that underwear you have on," Bunny whispered as she pulled Harriet's T-shirt off and cupped a small breast in

123

her hand. When she saw Harriet's shoulders tremble, she hugged her shyly. "It's all as new to me as it is to you, baby. Can't you help me out a little?" Her voice was thick with emotion as she sat down.

Tentatively, Harriet took Bunny's hand.

Bunny's fingers gently stroked Harriet's thighs. Trying to get Harriet to relax, she playfully snapped the elastic waistband of her shorts. "Getting kind of used to these, aren't you?"

"What are you doing, Bunny?" Harriet moved a few inches away.

"I want us to explore what we're both feeling. Look at me, tell me you're feeling the same."

Harriet turned to her, knowing she was incapable of expressing her feelings. Then Bunny leaned toward her, took her face between her hands and passionately kissed her.

Harriet pulled away and rolled over on her stomach. "I can't Bunny . . . I just can't."

Bunny paid no heed to Harriet's words. Instead, she teasingly traced the length of Harriet's body with her breasts, then lay upon her, her flesh molding itself to Harriet's. She began biting Harriet's neck, gently at first, then quick and hard with passion. As she lay down beside her, she rubbed Harriet's shoulders, the small of her back, her buttocks.

"You like this, don't you?" Bunny murmured. "You like my touching you this way."

Bunny tugged at her shorts. Harriet's hips rose and Bunny stripped the garment from her body. She continued to caress her, feeling unsure only in not knowing what to do next. "Don't hold back," Bunny said, "turn to me."

Now only a slight film of sweat separated their flesh. Harriet turned and with her body wiped that barrier away.

124

"I can't believe this is happening," Harriet sighed. "It's wonderful."

Bunny, giddy with emotion, reached out to touch Harriet, her hand moving toward the softness of golden curls. Harriet pulled her hand away. "You're as shy as I am," Bunny whispered fondly, "how lovely. But at least now we know how we feel about each other."

When Harriet didn't reply, Bunny began to caress her. She massaged her temples lightly, then ran circles across Harriet's forehead and cheeks. She blew kisses in her ears, kissed her lightly on the mouth, teased her with her tongue. Hungrily, Harriet returned the kiss and held Bunny in a tight embrace. A moment later, she abruptly took her arms away. Lying flat on the bed, she stretched her hands toward the sides of the mattress.

"You like what I'm doing, don't you?" Bunny queried. The answer she wanted was reflected in Harriet's eyes. Her lips grazed Harriet's shoulders and touched her breasts. She kissed each breast, lingering for long, delicious moments as Harriet murmured with pleasure at Bunny's sweet attention.

Bunny continued her lovemaking, waiting patiently for Harriet to respond, but Harriet's arms were still stretched out across the mattress, her hands clutching the sheets.

"Do you want me to stop?" Bunny asked.

"No," Harriet moaned, "everything you're doing, it's—"

"Then hold me, show me you want me. Love isn't a game for one."

"I know, Harriet said, "I just prefer . . . I'd just rather—"

"You'd rather what? What about me?"

When Harriet didn't answer, Bunny abruptly moved away. She reached for her robe. "I'm going outside."

Disappointed and angry, wanting to be alone, Bunny

closed the French doors between the balcony and their bedroom.

So this is Harriet Pearl, she thought furiously. Doesn't she think I have any feelings? I can't believe she could just . . . lay there . . . and expect me to just . . . ravish her.

Then Bunny laughed out loud. Ravish her? Where am I? In a tropical island movie, or on an assignment—or where? But she's *Mr*. Pearl. *I'm* the Mrs. I deserve some attention, don't I?

As comical as the situation was, and as frustrating, Bunny was suddenly overcome with sadness. Harriet, we never planned on this . . . maybe I expected too much.

She sat alone looking out at the night sky, hurt and disappointed. I risked as much as she did . . . more. She wasn't fair . . .

Then she heard the door open.

"Bunny, I'm sorry," Harriet began.

"No apologies, Harriet, not now. Save them for to-morrow. Or forget them. Maybe we were both mistaken. Just go back to bed, leave me alone."

"I will. When you come back to bed with me."

"I don't like mental games—"

"I'm not playing games, Bunny." Harriet knelt down at Bunny's side, the robe she'd put on slipping lightly from her shoulders. She took Bunny's hands in her own. "I was afraid because I'm in love with you, Bunny. Don't you know that?"

When Bunny didn't answer, Harriet rose, took her in her arms and held her. "Let me make love to you," Harriet whispered, her hands touching Bunny with a trembling gentleness that Bunny had never felt before. Then her caresses became urgent and demanding.

As Harriet's passion washed over her, her hot breath

filling Bunny like a sail, moving her on a course for which there was no chart, Bunny sighed with pleasure.

"Please," Harriet whispered, "please come with me. Please."

She took Bunny's hand, led her back into the room and toward the bed. She eased Bunny's body back onto the sheet, placing a pillow beneath her head.

"Tell me . . . show me what you like," Harriet said with urgency.

Bunny guided Harriet's hand over her breasts and down her stomach. "Touch me," she said, "touch me inside."

Harriet's movements were awkward and tentative at first but soon she began to follow Bunny's rhythms.

"Go deeper," Bunny cried in ecstasy, "Feel me, move with me."

Thrilled and amazed, Harriet responded to Bunny's frenzied need with the heat of her own passion. She lost herself in the wonder of Bunny, adoring Bunny's touch on her as she caressed and devoured her. She merged with Bunny's currents, moving to their source, tasting the sweet juices of Bunny's body, feeling her tense and rise and fall and tense and rise again.

Harriet held Bunny tightly, she felt the power of Bunny's orgasm as Bunny's cries brought tears welling to her own eyes. When had she given such pleasure? When had she known such passion? Never.

Bunny eased Harriet up beside her and Harriet wrapped her legs around Bunny's body. She moved back and forth as she continued to caress Bunny, but now ever, ever so gently.

"It was good?" Harriet asked tentatively, wanting to hear that she had pleased Bunny.

There was no answer. The silence was unbearable for

Harriet. She nibbled Bunny's shoulder. "It *was* good, wasn't it?"

Bunny touched Harriet's face lovingly. "I love you," she whispered.

Harriet sighed with contentment, feeling a closeness she had never known before. Then slowly, her mood began to change. She stroked Bunny's thigh, then pinched her playfully. "Come on, don't keep me in suspense. Did I disappoint you, Bun?" she asked imploringly.

Bunny laughed. "Surely you jest." Then she pushed Harriet's own body away and with a sudden movement straddled her waist. She reached out and with open hands pressed down on Harriet's shoulders. "Let me look at you," she said. Her eyes took in Harriet from the waist up, then she slid down beside her and scanned the length of Harriet's body.

The small breasts were firm and perfectly shaped, and Bunny's fingertips grazed their hardened nipples, then passed over Harriet's thin waist and lean, beautiful thighs. She reached as far down Harriet's long legs as she could, tickling her calves.

Harriet, her eyes still glazed from lovemaking, looked shyly at Bunny. "Love me," she whispered.

"Oh but I do," Bunny answered. "And I know exactly what you want right now. I can feel it."

"Can you?" Harriet asked wondrously.

"Yes, sweets, I can."

She gave Harriet's buttocks a playful squeeze, then tightened her grasp. She nipped Harriet's breasts.

"You like it to hurt just a little, don't you?" Bunny implored.

"Just a little," Harriet answered, "not too much . . . "

"No . . . not too much," Bunny answered huskily.

Harriet's hands gripped Bunny's shoulders. "Make me

come," she murmured, "make me really come. Please . . . please . . . "

"Hush, love, don't worry. You'll come . . . all you want . . . What do you think of that?"

Quickly, Bunny's mouth moved over Harriet's body, exploring all of her, not missing an inch, leaving love bites wherever her passion took her. Then Bunny's tongue found Harriet, and moved in and out, slowly, ever so slowly against the softness of her pink flesh.

Harriet was drawn into a current she had never known and a coming that seemed to have no end.

From their bed Harriet watched a morning star fade from sight, the pale grey sky a sudden broad expanse of rosy hues. She spoke to Bunny knowing that she too was awake. "Morning," she said softly. She kissed Bunny, brushing back strands of hair that had fallen across her face; then she propped herself up on an elbow and looked down at her partner.

"How about coffee and a smoke?" she asked.

"Sounds good," Bunny murmured, "just make sure it's a cigarette and not one of those Cuban cigars."

Harriet laughed, then stretched lazily before she got out of bed. Minutes later she sat down on the edge of the bed and offered Bunny a cup of coffee.

They smiled at each other. "Taste all right?" Harriet asked.

"Never better," Bunny said. "Here, want one of these?" She passed the cigarettes to Harriet and held the lighter for her as Harriet inhaled.

"Thanks," Harriet said, taking Bunny's hand. "You know, I think the cigars are wearing pretty thin on me . . . and so is Harry."

"I couldn't agree with you more," Bunny replied. "You make a much better woman than a man. Come here, lover." Bunny's arms opened wide. Harriet met her embrace as if she'd known it all her life. She lay comfortably in the nest of Bunny's arms as Bunny stroked her forehead and ran her fingers through Harriet's blonde curls.

"I hope you mean what you're saying," Harriet said.

"Oh I do. I mean all the things I say . . . all the things I said last night."

"You're sure it's not Harry you want?" Harriet asked.

"Pretty sure," Bunny said teasingly. "You were wonderful last night . . . you're wonderful now."

"We have a lot to talk about, don't we?"

"Yes," Bunny said.

Bunny's tone was surprisingly serious. Wanting to see her expression, Harriet tried to sit up but Bunny held her close.

"Good thing we're in the middle of this case," she continued, "otherwise we might be tempted to get into some pretty heavy soul searching. Luckily we won't have time—"

"We've time for each other," Harriet said, lightly kissing Bunny's breasts, "that's all I care about."

"Is it?"

"What do you think? As long as our priorities are straight, we'll be okay."

Bunny smiled. "Nothing's straight now, lover. The job *has* to come first, you know that, don't you?"

"I suppose so, but I never felt less like thinking about work than I do right now."

"That could be dangerous for both of us," Bunny replied as she held Harriet tight, "but I know just what you mean."

In his air-conditioned Manhattan office, Stillwell waited to hear from Harriet. Harry Pearl's routine business calls were being rerouted from Ohio to New York and conversations between Harriet and himself were in code. Though the two agents had been on Los Pagos for nearly three weeks, they had yet to provide him with any hard evidence against Turner.

Stillwell felt vague uneasiness about Harriet's approach to the assignment. Though she was following assigned procedures as instructed, her usual serious, businesslike manner had, of late, became light, almost euphoric. Must be the heat, he thought. Who could maintain a steady head in those temperatures?

I should talk to the other one to see what's really going on, he mused. Thoughts of Bunny produced a wave of emotion he did not want to explore, and he was relieved as the sharp ring of the phone cut the feeling off.

"Vic baby," the familiar voice teased, "how's my favorite accountant? Watching my new investments grow while your boss wilts his ass on Los Pagos?"

Who the hell did she think she was talking to? He pressed his knuckles into his jawbone, rubbing the skin, feeling rough stubble. This role playing had gone too far. He needed to talk to Silver . . . Harriet'd had too much of the tropics.

Harriet began to speak in code about the guns that had been issued only yesterday to the police force. Russian-made guns. This was something new, and startling. Stillwell began to take notes. Then Harriet abruptly concluded the conversation saying she would check in the next day.

Stillwell's response was firm. "Don't bother, Mr. Pearl, everything's under control." Over Harriet's protests, Stillwell continued, "I'll get back to you the first of next week. Trust me to handle business as you would, sir." Then, nearly choking on his words, he added, "Mrs. Pearl said there'd be an extra week's vacation for me if she has you to herself now and then."

Harriet paused, but when she continued her voice was calm, even. "If that's what my wife promised you, I won't interfere. Will we speak Monday?"

"Yes," Stillwell replied, "in the morning, Mr. Pearl."

Stillwell rubbed the tip of his nose. Now where would Hosada be getting Russian guns? Cuba? El Salvador? Nicaragua? He'd never had any use for outsiders, there was no record of foreign intervention on Los Pagos at any time. Now there were plans for this casino . . . the island was being armed . . . and from what Pearl had said last week, the police were even wearing their uniforms.

Who was behind this? Hosada hadn't taken a step forward since he seized power. Was it his wife? That Lieutenant of his, Eduardo Gomez? Or was it Turner? What the hell was Turner doing on Los Pagos all this time? He'd already extended his leave from the Caracas office. For what?

Why did I ever send those women down there, he thought in frustration. They should have figured all this out by now. Lousy field agents, both of them.

Then he leaned back and thought for a few moments.

I'll tell Perry the girls are on to something so big that they need first-rate backup. Those two will never solve this without help. *I'll* go down, I'll show them what it means to be agents.

Wait till Bunny sees me in action . . . and if she plays her cards right, I'll let her find out what a real man is all about.

Maybe I *was* taken out of the field because of this bum leg, but it's not going to stop me now. They need supervision . . . they need my help. I'll tell Perry I'm taking the first available flight out.

He hadn't felt this excited in years. He called Perry's secretary and requested a brief meeting within the hour.

The old ceiling paddle fan whirled, moving the dense tropical air. Bunny fanned out her hair, enjoying the coolness of the breeze, the swirling blades feeling like an oversized comb. She arched her neck, patting her skin with a dampened towel. The weather had been hot and sticky these past few days though rain had been promised all week. Is it ever going to fall, she wondered.

She arched her eyebrows and pouted at Harriet, then blew her a kiss. Harriet blew one back as she continued her conversation with Stillwell, telling him about the Russian-made guns they'd observed being carried by Hosada's police.

In a red silk teddy, Bunny reclined against the pillows, then knelt seductively at the end of the bed. Trying to break Harriet up, she wriggled her fanny.

"Give the boss . . . my best," she said in her best Mae West imitation, "Tell him we're . . . working . . . every hour of the day. And night as well."

Harriet muttered a fast goodbye to Stillwell and Bunny collapsed as Harriet tackled her from the rear.

"Want to get me in trouble with the big cheese, don't you?" Harriet threw her robe on the floor. She covered Bunny's body with quick, hungry kisses.

"No more, Harriet," Bunny cried out, "no more, we're being bad."

"Bad?" Harriet asked, "what do you mean?"

Bunny moved away, slipped off the bed, stretched like a lazy, well-contented cat, then sat back in a wicker rocking chair. "Don't look so serious, love."

"What are we doing that's so *bad?*" Harriet asked. "I love you, is that bad?"

"Not at all, my darling. What's bad is that you just about hung up in Stillwell's ear when you caught sight of my sweet little . . . derriere."

"I did not. If you want to know what was going on, Stillwell informed me that he doesn't want any contact from us until next week. Would you have felt better if I'd ignored you?"

"Do you think you could?" Bunny said. She smiled seductively as she rocked back and forth waiting for a response from Harriet.

Harriet reached out and pulled her back to the bed as Bunny wrapped her arms around Harriet's waist, kissed her on the mouth, and said, "Try it."

"There are other things I'd like to try right now," Harriet said. She leaned back, looked tenderly at Bunny, and eased the silken strap of her teddy off her shoulders.

Bunny, sitting upright, the teddy rising over her thighs, moved no closer to Harriet. "Pleasure before business?" she asked.

"Just for a few minutes, Bunny. We have the rest of the day for work."

"What's on your mind?" Bunny asked curiously.

"I just want us to be close," Harriet said, passion growing in her eyes.

"Darling, we are," Bunny replied fervently.

"I want you," Harriet said. "Now."

Above the bed, the paddle fan made its lazy circle, round and round, the dull hum of the motor the only sound in the room. Soft breezes seem to push Harriet closer to Bunny. She ran her fingertips lightly over the silk teddy, tracing the lace pattern which covered her breasts.

Bunny moved closer, took Harriet's hand in her own,

134

kissed the palm and fingers, brought the hand back to her body. "I love the way you touch me," Bunny said in a husky voice.

Harriet caressed Bunny, touched her breasts, buried her head in Bunny's lap. The sensuousness of the silk against her face was so arousing that she groaned. She pulled Bunny down beside her, kissing her hair, her neck, her back. She held Bunny in her arms, slowly moving her body against the silk. Then Bunny turned around and took Harriet's face in her hands. Seeing desire so alive in Harriet's eyes, she kissed her, held her close, then helped Harriet to ease the silk teddy from her body.

The paddle fan whirled slowly, gentle breezes cooled the room, the women spoke of love.

Later, time took on its usual focus, though while making love that afternoon, Bunny felt that time had no meaning beyond the present moments with Harriet.

"Darling, I love you *so*," Bunny said as she and Harriet lay peacefully together. "We're just so good for each other."

"I know. It's wonderful." Harriet replied.

"Oh, it's more than that," Bunny said as she smiled contentedly. "And isn't it nice that we don't have to be in touch with Stillwell till next week? Wonder why? The next thing we know he'll be showing up *here*."

"Where would you get that idea?" Harriet said, propping herself up in bed.

"We're not doing our job, Pearl, that's why."

"Oh, back to business," Harriet said defensively. "I don't care for your tone just now, you're sounding too much like the old Bunny."

"I don't mean to—and I don't mean to upset you either. Now what's the matter?"

"I don't think there *is* much going on around here,"

135

Harriet said. "I'm sure Turner's involved with the purchasing of these new guns, but that's no world threat—"

Bunny sat up. In a sharp voice, she interrupted, "Anytime a United States diplomat is providing the means by which a foreign government—no matter how small—can buy Russian arms, *and* anticipates profit from a money making scheme like this casino—"

"I know, I know, you're right, Bunny. The man's turned traitor. I just don't feel like being super agent these days. I just feel . . . in love."

She continued in a serious voice, "What more can we do? We haven't had a single chance to investigate the island on our own, the way we should. There's always a shadow at our side. We might as well be prisoners on Los Pagos."

"Should that stop us?"

"How can it not? But the General's not hiding anything from us—Maria isn't either."

"Don't be so trusting. And why the constant chaperones?" Bunny challenged.

"Turner's idea, I'm sure. What if we do start looking around and get caught? We'll blow the setup before we have any hard evidence."

"We'll have to chance it," Bunny said, "we've been here for too long without finding anything out. We can't stall the Hosadas about the investment money much longer. Harriet, how are guns getting to the island? Who's the contact? Where are they being stored? How large *is* the military police? Aren't you curious?"

"Of course, but what are we supposed to do? Hoof it? I've tried to get a car a half dozen times—it's always the same story. We can have the car *and* one of Hosada's aides as the driver. We did that last week and what did we find out? Nothing—"

"That was before we noticed the guns. I know Stillwell is going to bust his butt to get down here, figure things out *real* fast and show us up."

"Perry won't go for that," Harriet said, wanting to change the subject.

"Really? He went for this husband and wife team, didn't he?"

"And aren't you glad he did?" Realizing that Bunny wasn't about to be deterred, Harriet said, "All right, Silver, let's go for it. I want to solve this case as badly as you do and I'm ready to do it now. I want to get home, I want us to plan our future—"

"You think I don't want that, too?"

"All *right!* And what *are* we going to do when we get back?"

"I want you to meet my mother," Bunny said, smiling, taking Harriet's hand.

"How nice, what else?"

"We have to decide who gives up which apartment."

"That's easy," Harriet said, "I've never liked my place—it's too small. And we might want to think about our future with CSW."

"We'll be senior agents when we break this case. The future looks fine, babe. Don't you agree?"

"Of course I do. I want to wrap this case up as much as you do," she added with conviction. "We'll take a chance in the next few days, time things right so no one becomes suspicious. We should be able to get lost for a couple of hours ... somehow. When I contact Stillwell next week, we'll have *facts* for him—specific information he can file in that tin cabinet of a head. I want him to know we're on top of this case. I want us to go back in glory."

"Then that's the way we're going!" Bunny replied with fervor.

Wearing bright Hawaiian shorts and a light sweat shirt, Harriet was engrossed in a series of rigorous stretching exercises. In the past three days, they still hadn't made any progress with the case, she thought disappointedly. How much longer before they got some answers? Then Bunny burst into the room, and Harriet hopped up, smiled, reached out for her.

Bunny shook her head as she tried to catch her breath. She sat down. Her lower lip protruding, she blew puffs of air up over her pink cheeks trying to brush back damp wisps of hair which fell across her forehead.

"I thought you were reading in the General's garden, Bun, not jogging. Especially in a sundress—"

"No time for jokes, Harriet, we're about to close in, we've got what we need. All you have to do is—"

"What are you talking about?" Harriet interrupted.

"I just overheard a conversation between Maria and Lars Hansen—"

"Lars Hansen?"

"Lars Hansen—yes, yes—the most notorious gun runner in the CIA's South American files. The one linked with Castro in the sixties, then with Papa Doc in Haiti. Now he's here."

"Are you *sure* it's Hansen?"

"We've seen his photo often enough," Bunny gasped. "I'd recognize that face anywhere. Harriet, he was threatening Maria. He said he can't wait any longer to be paid for the supplies he delivered."

"The Russian guns, of course," Harriet said excitedly.

138

"We've got to find out the size of that arsenal and where the hell those weapons are being stored! Maria apparently had a hard time coming up with the money—she gave Hansen a story about how long it takes to transfer funds from the general treasury, but the payment's going to be made this morning. Turner's about to deliver the cash! He's the contact between Hansen and the Hosadas! They're going to meet in the square in thirty minutes! Harriet, how fast can you run?"

"A mile in ten minutes when the terrain's ideal—which this isn't—"

"You've *got* to do it. The square's a good three mile hike. Get going, grab the telescopic lens for your camera. Here, throw it in this backpack. *Move,* Harriet. We'll have all the evidence we need within the hour!"

"If we're lucky," Harriet replied. "And what about Maria? The way she keeps tabs on us, she'll know something's up."

"No she won't. I'll be in the garden when she comes looking for me. I can't wait to tell her the plot of this novel, it's *so* exciting. And when she gets around to asking for you, I'll tell her you're out for your usual morning jog. She knows your routine as well as I do by now."

"Not all of it, I hope," Harriet said. She zipped up the backpack and gave Bunny a quick kiss goodbye.

Reaching the crest of the dirt road, Harriet felt as if she were floating. Perspiration blurred her vision, her muscles were tight, her heart was a flurry of drum beats against her chest. She wondered what her time was. She'd never run faster, that much she knew.

Ahead was the town square. She jogged on, thankful that she could slow her pace. She wiped the sweat from her

139

eyes and then laughed in exhilaration as she saw Alan Turner sitting at the outdoor cafe with a man in army fatigues whom she recognized as Lars Hansen.

The best thing to do, she decided, was to keep running in case they'd noticed her, then backtrack through the brush for the photos.

Minutes later, she scurried up a steep hillside and positioned herself in the midst of thick foliage. What a view, and with this lens she could photograph how much sugar they put in their coffee.

Time passed. She recorded their movements but nothing of interest was happening. Had a transaction already taken place?

Then Turner handed an envelope to Hansen and for brief seconds the camera snapped a series of photos of money being counted.

"Pay dirt, Bunny, we've hit it!" Harriet shouted as she continued to snap away.

With this evidence, Harriet thought, he'll be found guilty of collaboration in any courtroom in the United States. He'll be arrested when he first steps foot on American soil, including the American consulate in Venezuela. Bunny, we've done it!

When Hansen tucked the money away and the two men returned to their coffee, Harriet capped the lens, carefully placed the camera in the bag and began the jaunt back to Bunny.

As if nothing at all had happened, Harriet jogged up to Bunny who was reading under the shade of flowering bougainvillea.

"Any chance I can read that when you're finished," she asked, "or have you already promised it to someone?"

"Maria's a fast reader, Harry, you'll get it soon."

"I'm fast at a few things myself," Harriet said with

pride. "You might say today was my personal best. Aren't you going to congratulate me?"

Bunny jumped up from her chair, quickly looked about to see if they were being observed, then excitedly said, "You bet I am!" She put her arms around Harriet's neck and kissed her resoundingly on the lips. "Way to go, partner! I want to hear all about it, *after* we call Stillwell—"

"We *can't*, remember? We won't hear from him before the first of the week."

"Damn! Just when we need to talk. We'll put the call through to Ohio anyway, and if we don't get a response from him in the next forty-eight hours, we're going to have to risk placing a call to Sam Perry."

VIII

Stillwell boarded the small charter plane that twice
weekly made the short run from Trinidad to Los Pagos.
The islands were twenty miles apart and on days when the
charter didn't make its jaunt, tourists and islanders alike
made their way to Los Pagos on the mail boat, the *Maria
Ana*. At his hotel the previous night, Stillwell had inquired
about transportation between the two islands, and the
plane had been strongly recommended. After seeing the
ancient fishing vessel tied to its mooring, bobbing in the
gentle swells of the evening tide, he could see why. Still, he
was somewhat surprised to see that the eight passenger
Cessna Cardinal prop plane was full.

There's no place off the beaten track anymore, he
thought as he secured the seatbelt for takeoff. From his

window seat, he soon surveyed the sparkling emerald sea and a small fishing fleet sailing north from Trinidad. He wondered what their catch would be. And how about his? What would he bring back?

At the Los Pagos airport Stillwell picked up his bags and walked in the direction of a small van. He'd been told it was the only means of public transportation to the Sand Pebble Guest House where he had reserved a room. How, he wondered, would he get about on the island?

While he registered at the guest house, he tried to engage the desk clerk in conversation but the man's only response was a tired, thin smile.

Then the owner of the Sand Pebble appeared, a tall, heavyset man who wore white shorts, a batik print shirt. "Mr. Stillwell," he said, "our American guest, welcome."

Stillwell extended a hand to his large, friendly host who escorted him to the corner room on the first floor. Surprised at how cool the room was, he noticed that dark shades had been drawn and a ceiling fan hummed above his head. On a white wooden table sat a pitcher of ice water and tall glasses. The host filled a glass and handed it to Stillwell.

"Drink often, señor, and rest during the afternoon. You are here to relax, no?"

"Of course," Stillwell said, "but I want to get about the island, too ... do as much sight-seeing as I can."

His host chuckled. "That will be very easy," he said. "I will give you a tour myself. I will take you fishing if you like. You may join my family and me for dinner—"

"What I'd really like," Stillwell curtly interrupted, "is a car. I'd like to rent a car and take my own time exploring. Is that possible?"

"I am sorry, señor, but there are not many vehicles on this part of the island. Few people have the need for an automobile on Los Pagos. The main road which circles the island," he apologized, " is in bad repair."

Stillwell frowned. "I've got to have a car," he insisted.

"You are welcome to use my motor scooter—"

"I've got a bum leg, that's why I need the car. But if your scooter's got an electric starter, it'll do," Stillwell conceded as he set down the glass.

"Of course. It is the latest model Honda via Caracas. It arrived only last month."

"Yeah? And I can use it?"

"As my guest, I would be honored."

"Thanks, but let me pay you."

The host only shook his head and reached into his pants pocket for the key. "Wait until tomorrow before you begin sight-seeing, spend today with us. Lunch will be served in an hour. Until then, rest, Mr. Stillwell. There are no urgent concerns on Los Pagos."

Stillwell hung up his suit, took off his shirt and poured himself another glass of water. He thought: I'll find out all I need to now from Charming Charlie at lunch, then I'll take a spin around this end of the island. Why wait? I've got work to do.

He stretched out on the bed and watched large flies circling around the air currents produced by the fan. Small spiders climbed across the stucco walls, birds and various insects made a racket outside the window, a dog barked. Stillwell closed his eyes, but he didn't sleep.

I'm wired, he thought. I can *taste* action. Wait till those two see me. Got to get them alone first so they don't blow the whole cover. Maybe I'll catch Bunny at the beach, see what she looks like in one of those bikinis. Sneak up on her, pinch her ass, then step back while it sinks in who's here.

He laughed out loud at the expression he envisioned on

Bunny's face. Eagerly he anticipated the unfolding of what he knew would be great adventure.

That afternoon he took the scooter out for a short ride. Tentative about the speed of the bright red Honda, he did his best to avoid deep ruts in the dirt road; he didn't want to take any spills. As he'd expected after driving only a short distance, the bumpy terrain began to aggravate his bad leg. This would be a slow ride.

To all appearances, he had no purpose in mind other than touring the island. He didn't deviate from his slow, steady speed, except for taking a closer look at what he knew from photographs was General Hosada's Palace. I'll get the guided tour another time, he thought.

He knew he was making headway circling the southern end of the island. Forty minutes later, as he approached the high bluffs at the western tip, he decided to take in the scenic view. He pulled in under the shade of a large tree, took out his thermos, drank the cold water, then splashed some on his perspiring face. Got to give this leg a break from these goddamn roads, he thought.

It was late afternoon when he motored into the town square. He noticed a young woman at a concession stand selling bottles of chilled Spanish beer from an old Coca-Cola cooler filled with block ice. You work up a hell of a thirst in this heat, he thought as he parked the scooter and walked toward her. He paid for the beer, sat down at a table, and stretched his legs out, rubbing the joint connected to his prosthesis.

Sore as hell already, wouldn't you know. So what? He'd put in a good day's work. He'd catch up on his sleep tonight, be a new man in the morning. Not much doing here.

Then he saw a group of young men walking his way. As they gathered in the square, he observed their uniforms. As any tourist might do, Stillwell got up and casually strolled their way. Their khaki uniforms weren't new, but they were clean, starched and ironed razor sharp so that trouser creases stood out and old boots glistened with reflections. Hosada's military police, Stillwell knew, noting their youth and strength.

Then he noticed their guns. Pearl and Silver were right, their guns were Russian made.

The group was approached by an older man, grey-haired, grizzled, intense. He began to speak to one of the young officers, jabbing his finger at him with authority.

I know mercenaries when I see them, Stillwell thought. What's this SWAT team being trained for? It sure as hell isn't traffic control. This could be a bigger operation than I figured.

When the General awakened, he called for Maria. His aide, bringing the usual breakfast tray, told him that she was still at morning prayers. Patiently, the old man sipped his morning coffee and waited for her return.

Dressed in white, she soon entered his room, prayer book and rosary in hand.

"Did you have much to confess, my pet? Did the holy father scold you?" he asked playfully.

"No, Papa, my soul is pure," she replied. She smiled and kissed him lightly. "Almost pure," she added.

Taking her hand, kissing it tenderly, he said, "I'm glad you've returned. I wanted to see you before I leave the Palace this morning. I feel weary . . . I need some relaxation, Maria. Eduardo, Alan and I will fish in my private streams today. It has been a long time since I have enjoyed that pleasure. I put Harry Pearl and his wife in your hands. Will you find some pleasant diversion for them?"

146

"Of course. But will you be gone all day?"

"Perhaps. And why not? This is a day to savor. Our goal has been achieved ... The Americans *will* be our investors. Harry Pearl has assured me a half million in good faith money will arrive next week, another three and a half million next month. *Think* of how long we have searched, Maria. Finally," he said with satisfaction, "Alan Turner has been of some use to us."

"And the Pearls as well," she said, pleased that all was going well.

"Yes, I would have invited Harry Pearl to join us today but I want to make sure that all is clearly understood between Turner and me. I don't want him to become greedy, to aspire for more than has been agreed upon. I want Eduardo present as all of this is reviewed. Do you understand, Maria? Eduardo is my successor—"

"Don't speak that way, Papa," Maria said sharply.

"Why not? I will not live forever. But I *will* live to see our dream achieved," he said with assurance. "Come to me, Maria, sit beside me for a moment."

Tenderly, he put his arm around her. "You must not fear my death, Maria. Often I have told you that I will know when my time has come. This is not cause for sorrow, though it would be lovely to sit high on this peak forever, just the two of us."

Maria looked at her husband with affection. "Papa, you look so happy," she said fondly.

Intent on gathering as much information as he could, Stillwell had spent the three days following his arrival on Los Pagos observing the comings and goings at the General's Palace. He'd decided against letting his agents know he was on the island. Earlier that morning he had placed a call to

147

Perry's office with instructions for Pearl should she try to reach him.

"Tell her I've been called out of town on a personal emergency," he had said. "I'll contact her on Monday as planned."

He smiled to himself. He'd seen the Pearls several times, of course, through his high-powered binoculars. A couple of regular love-birds, he thought. When I circulate those shots of them walking hand in hand, embracing even, on the beach, they'll be the joke of the Agency. What dingbats. While they're billing and cooing at each other, I'll nail this case.

He stepped from behind lush foliage into the small clearing overlooking the Palace. Turner, General Hosada and Eduardo, dressed casually and carrying fishing gear, walked toward a jeep.

Think I'll just head on down to the pier, Stillwell decided. He'd already noticed the presidential yacht, a two-deck Chris-Craft power boat ideal for deep sea fishing or pleasure cruising.

Soon he sat at an outdoor café near the dock and waited for the official entourage, curious as to who else might have joined the fishing party. But there was no one, he saw, as the jeep pulled up to the pier. He watched Eduardo help the General down the swaying wooden dock while Turner shouldered the fishing gear.

A few minutes later the General's craft pulled away from the dock, cutting through the calm waters of the harbor. Stillwell watched it fade beyond the vanishing point, then he left the café and walked to his scooter.

It looked like he had the morning to himself. Why not check out that tin warehouse near the airport?

He had spotted the warehouse the day before. It was located on a winding, narrow dirt road, an offshoot from the main road near the airport. He'd observed a dozen of Hosada's military police being put through their paces by what he figured was yet another mercenary. He'd take another ride out there, try to get a look. If it was a depot for weapons and ammo as he suspected, maybe he could figure out who Turner's source was.

A short time later, he pulled the scooter off the road and into the bushes. As he was about to make his way to the building, an old military truck bounced down the road, its cargo members of Hosada's police force once again.

Maybe I'll get the illustrated tour from right here, he thought. But though he waited patiently while the men went through a series of assault maneuvers, no one approached the warehouse.

So they were here for the day. He'd head back to town. As he pushed the scooter to the main road, his stump began to hurt. He parked the scooter on its kick-stand and reached into a khaki bag for his screwdriver.

Christ, why did he have to have an above the knee amputation? What a pain in the ass. Impatiently he pulled up his trouser leg. When he got back, he'd have to have the center bolt realigned—the dirt roads and the scooter were playing too much havoc with it.

He adjusted and tightened the bolt securely; he couldn't take a chance on losing it. The hinged prosthesis had already lost some of its flexibility and he felt uneasy about it. Mind over matter, he told himself, but he winced as once more he put his full weight on the limb.

The General knew the exact spot he wanted to fish. It was at a bend in the stream, marked by a hairpin curve. As a young man he'd come there often, walking down the village's dusty road which quickly became nothing more than a path cut between the bushes. In years past, the journey was arduous, taking the better part of the morning; yet the fishing was always good. He never returned to his family without a large catch.

He hadn't walked that way in over forty years, he reflected, wondering if any of the young villagers today followed the path he had cut so long ago.

"Eduardo," he called, "cut your speed. I want to enjoy the view." He leaned back in his chair enjoying the shade afforded by the lush foliage growing on both sides of the stream. "Alan, I promise you a fine day of fishing."

"I'm sure it will be, General," Turner replied.

"You like to fish, Turner?"

"Yes, of course."

"I wasn't sure," said Hosada, "but I thought we needed the time for . . . conversation. We have much to celebrate. We will soon enjoy the good fortune brought to us all by Mr. and Mrs. Pearl."

The General observed the thin smile on Turner's lips, the lazy grin on Eduardo's face. My companions, he thought, in an ambitious, risky venture. Mr. Turner, though I have not told you yet, soon it will be time for you to bring your holiday on our island to a close. I cannot risk what I think you hope to gain—greater fortune and the loyalty of Señora Hosada.

He gazed at Eduardo. I wish you were cunning, clever, a man of intelligence. You are a plodder, nothing more, but such men have their place in history. You will follow my plans without question.

Pity you and Maria have no liking for each other. That will have to change. When Turner is gone, I think it will. Maria will become your wife and one day the two of you will produce an heir to all that I have created.

"A pleasant journey," the General said aloud, "a pleasant

150

day." Ahead he could see the sharp bend in the stream. "We're there, Eduardo," he called. "Drop anchor as soon as we approach the bend."

Anxious to begin fishing, deciding to postpone business matters until after lunch, the General reached for one of his rods. From the bait bucket he plucked a fat blood worm and pierced it with the metal hook. "I will catch a handful of these beauties today," he said as he stood and, with an expert turn of the wrist, cast his line.

He smiled as birds flew up from the calm waters of the stream, startled by this intrusion. We'll be gone by sundown, he thought, we won't be in your way for long.

He forgot Turner, Eduardo, even Maria for these golden moments. Then suddenly, feeling tired, ever so tired, he sank back into his chair, closed his eyes, the image of birds in flight ever present in his mind.

Seated at the bow, Eduardo reached into his bait bucket for a worm. He wasn't having much luck this morning. Maybe it was the worms, he thought. He dropped one into the palm of his hand and watched it crawl toward his thumb. As it looped itself over the thumb, Eduardo grasped it between his two hands, stretching the worm, pulling it. Then he dropped it to the deck of the boat and watched it crawl away.

He almost laughed aloud thinking of how Maria Hosada would have to crawl for him when the General was no longer her husband. She thinks *she* will rule the island, while this American has dreams of owning us all. *I* will rule. I will seize power quickly. With Lars Hansen agreeing to continue supplying weapons and ammunition—that's all I need. Maria will be helpless.

With his fishing rod, he dragged the worm back within

151

his grasp, picked it up, and angrily tore it in half. He threw the wriggling pieces over the side of the boat and leaned back in satisfaction.

Though he'd caught no fish, Turner found the day's activities pleasant enough. Enjoying the late morning air, he felt content. Finally, things were beginning to go his way.

What a stroke of luck to have come upon the Pearls. He'd begun to think he'd never find a backer for the old despot. Now the project would move ahead—and quickly.

He gazed at the General. Look at him . . . he's slept most of the morning. He's fishing for dreams, not trout.

Turner smiled as he saw the General's rod bend, the line tighten. "I'll be damned," he said, "he's going to catch one." He looked toward Eduardo. "Why don't you come down and lend a hand?"

Eduardo grunted, propped his rod into the holder and lumbered down the narrow steps from the top deck.

"What do you have there, General?" he asked.

"He's sleeping, Eduardo. Wake him so he knows what's going on."

Eduardo touched the General on the shoulder. "Hey, General Hosada, you've got a fish," he said in a loud voice. "You've done better than both of us." Gently he shook the chair and as he did, the old man's rod fell to the deck. His huge head slumped on his chest, his arms fell to his side.

"Turner, help me."

Gently, they eased the General's body to the deck. Turner checked for a pulse but he knew from the General's slack grey face that he was dead.

"Cover the body," he said. "Let's get back to shore."

Eduardo looked at Turner. "What?" he asked dully. "Why?"

"Can't you see for yourself, Eduardo?" Turner turned and walked away.

Dazed, Eduardo knelt on the deck. He opened the General's shirt and placed his hand over the heart praying he would find life. Then he took off his jacket and covered the old man tenderly. He held the General's hand in his own, stroking the tanned, wrinkled skin now so quickly growing cold. Tears filled his eyes. He leaned his head back against the cabin and wept.

"I offer my condolences," Turner said.

Eduardo opened his eyes and looked at the Consul.

"I'm sorry," Turner continued, "let me help you. I know the sorrow you must feel."

The words spoken by Turner were correct, the tone of his voice offered the proper sympathy. Then why, Eduardo thought, did his eyes glimmer with victory?

As he looked at Turner, the grief Eduardo felt was soon dispersed by a sudden awareness of the problems he now faced. He rubbed his forehead and reflected, pacing the deck.

Then he glanced down at the old man's body and the solution was apparent. He felt a heady confidence swell within him. He smiled to himself, contemplating the future.

It's all so simple, he thought as he turned to face Turner. "We can't leave the General's body on deck," Eduardo said. "Help me carry it into the cabin, then we'll return to the Palace."

As they descended the few narrow stairs leading to the cabin, Eduardo concentrated on all he must accomplish in the next few hours.

He and Turner laid the body on the bed. Eduardo

gazed at the General in respect, thoughts racing through his mind. He crossed himself and in a choked whisper said a prayer.

"I'll be with you in a moment," Eduardo said in dismissal of Turner. "I want to make him presentable for his wife."

"Of course," Turner replied. "I'll gather my things."

Eduardo watched Turner as he walked back up to the deck, then he reached into a drawer for the pistol the General always kept there.

He stared at the General's peaceful face. You always boasted you would pick the time of your own death, old man. Unfortunately, destiny cheated you of that privilege. It might have been easier had you lived a while longer but we're certain to achieve success in any case. The money from the Pearls has already been promised. Should they show any signs of backing out, it will not be difficult to convince them otherwise. But Turner—Turner serves no purpose. I can take no chances that he will not attempt to conspire against me.

As he thought of breaking the news of the General's death to Maria, his confidence began to diminish. How could he permit her to live, yet how could he do away with her?

And then he saw a way. He would drive immediately to the Palace, bring Maria—and Maria alone—back to the boat on the pretense that the General had fallen ill and Turner was ministering care. Once he had her back here . . .

By sundown, he would return to the Palace, assume the power rightfully his and with deep regret and sorrow announce the explosion that had caused the tragic accident that had taken the lives of General and Señora Hosada, and the American Consul. He would explain his own survival on the distance he had been blown from the yacht. He would

154

say that he had escaped without mishap and had been able to swim ashore.

He loaded the revolver, strapped the holster to his waist, pulled his shirt out over his trousers, and returned to the deck. Turner was sitting on a lounge chair, but he stood as Eduardo approached him.

"Death is quiet, is it not, Señor Turner?" Eduardo asked, noting the silence about them. "Not even the birds are singing."

"A still moment, Eduardo, I agree. Are we set for the return trip?"

"Nearly ready."

"Do you need any help?"

"Would you pull up the anchor?"

"It's as good as done," Turner replied as he walked to the bow of the yacht. He bent over and reached for the hempen line, but from the corner of his eye, he saw a glistening reflection in the afternoon sun.

He straightened and turned to face Eduardo and the revolver which was aimed at him. Turner's blood turned to ice. "What do you think you are going to do? Murder an American consul? You'll never get away with it."

Boldly he stepped toward him, held out his hand as if to take the gun. "I know you're upset by the General's death. Let me help you."

Eduardo shook his head, a slight smile on his lips. "It is you who need help. Say your prayers, Consul."

Turner dropped his hand to his side, looked at Eduardo in disbelief, then in frozen horror as the gun barrel rose and focused on his head. The sharp crack of the gun shattered the still air.

The Pearls and Maria sat in the Palace sunporch. Maria was restless. An hour ago she had had a premonition that a

155

tragedy had occurred. To whom, she asked herself. Where? Is it the General?

As she gazed at the bright blue sea, a large cloud swept across the horizon and blotted out the sun. The room itself was cloaked in darkness. She felt something touch her shoulder and turned quickly. Neither Bunny nor Harry Pearl were near her.

She looked for kindred expressions from the Pearls, but they were gazing at each other, lost in thoughts of love. Annoyed, she turned away and wondered when the General and Alan would return from their fishing trip. Come to think of it, why this sudden impulse to fish the distant streams feeding the waters surrounding the bay of Los Pagos?

They talk about designing women, she thought angrily. Men are the real masters of the game, women have only refined it.

She was growing weary of her part in the intrigue between herself and the two men. No, three men, counting Eduardo, that dolt. She must never underestimate him because of his stupidity. That in itself could be the cause of great harm.

Why did Papa think she would take Eduardo as her husband? Surely he must know her better than that.

She laughed to herself, thinking that one man was worse than the other. Papa, Eduardo, Alan ... They all wanted this casino so badly ... But for very different reasons.

Maria turned back to the Pearls. "It's getting late, I don't understand why the General and Alan haven't returned from their fishing trip."

Harriet sensed the concern in Maria's voice and wanting to calm her anxieties, turned the conversation to the subject of investments.

156

"Perhaps we're to blame, Maria," Harriet said in as matter-of-fact a tone as she could muster. "Alan is probably trying to assure the General that we are reliable investors."

Maria dismissed the comment with an icy stare. "The General consults no one on matters of importance on this island—except me. Something else is in the air. It has nothing to do with the two of you."

Harriet stepped to Bunny's side and sat down beside her. She took Bunny's hand and the two of them watched Maria pace the floor. She might be upset, Harriet thought, but she's not about to crumble. If we'd hear from Stillwell, we could wrap this case up so quickly. Maybe Bunny's right, maybe we should call Sam Perry. If there's no response by tomorrow night, we will.

"I'm sorry," Harriet said, "I was just assuming—"

"It's always hazardous to assume, Mr. Pearl."

What was she upset about, Harriet wondered.

The room fell into an eerie silence as Harriet watched Maria stare out at the sea. And there was no mistaking that as she stood by the open window, she was trembling.

Once back at the dock, Eduardo walked quickly to his jeep and began the short journey to the Palace. His foot floored the gas pedal, then let up, the uneven driving seeming to follow his muddled thoughts.

Though there was a pleasant ocean breeze blowing and the sun had paled behind banks of clouds, Eduardo's beefy body was covered with a glistening film of perspiration. His forehead and upper lip dripped beads of sweat. In frustration, he cursed himself, and what he now saw was his stupidity.

How could he get Maria out here without anyone else knowing about it? If he told her the General was ill, she'd bring a doctor. If he conveyed the simple message that he

157

wanted to see her, she'd be suspicious.

"How can I get that bitch out onto the boat?" he said aloud, taking a sharp corner of the dusty dirt road on two wheels.

He was taken by the sudden image of his own strength, the power he now possessed. He smiled with satisfaction, knowing that he would find a way.

As Eduardo entered the sun room, Maria looked up and scowled. "Where is my husband?" she asked in an agitated voice.

The expression of scorn on her face infuriated him. In as calm a voice as he could muster, he said, "The General has taken ill on the boat. He wants to see only one person. No others. Come quickly or it may be too late."

"Do you truly think I believe you?" she asked angrily. "What have you done to him?"

She threw herself against Eduardo's massive body, clawing his face with both hands.

He seized her wrists in his hands. "You're coming with me. Now."

In a sudden move, Harriet threw herself at Eduardo, grasping his hands, trying to free Maria. She aimed a kick at his groin.

"Bastard," Eduardo snarled, grabbing Harriet by the collar of her shirt. He twisted the fabric in his fist, and punched Harriet in the mouth.

Feeling warm blood run over her lips, Harriet did not try to protect herself. She stepped back, braced, took careful aim, and kicked Eduardo in the stomach. He threw a savage punch to her chest. She fell to the floor, clutching her body in pain. Bunny cried out as she ran toward Harriet.

158

"Stop where you are, Mrs. Pearl," Eduardo ordered, his revolver in his hand. "And you, Pearl, get up off the floor and into a chair. I want you all—the three of you—sitting over there against the wall. Do as I say—now!"

He waved the revolver at Maria and the Pearls. "Now," he shouted, "you'll listen to me. All of you."

"You've killed him, haven't you?" Maria accused. "You've killed your General."

"No! Never," Eduardo shouted. He laughed momentarily, then his expression grew serious. "Yes, the General is dead. I bring the news with sadness and regret. But his death was peaceful . . . I did not kill him."

"I don't believe you," Maria screamed. "Violence has occurred, I can feel it. Where is Alan? Why didn't he return with you?"

"That is a different story," Eduardo muttered. "There was an accident on board the boat."

"You murdered him, didn't you?"

"Why would I do that? Come with me and you will see for yourself."

"Maria," Bunny interrupted, "we're going with you. Don't you trust him—"

"Be quiet," Eduardo ordered. Then he realized he could not take Maria and leave the Pearls behind—nor could he take them all to the boat and be sure that he could control the situation. He needed time to think . . .

Harriet sat stunned and in pain. With one hand she held a handkerchief to her bleeding nose and mouth; with the other, she held her rib cage. Tears filled her eyes as she tried to breathe, each breath an exercise in pain.

Her voice breaking with grief, Maria said, "How could you come here and tell me of my husband's death so cruelly? How? You've known him all your life." She stared at him. "And why would you kill Turner?"

"Maria, how could he be allowed to live? I have to protect my own interests now. How secure would I be against you and Alan Turner?"

"You are naive, Eduardo," she replied with scorn. "You think there will be no retribution from the United States for the murder of the Consul?"

Eduardo's eyes shifted from Maria to the Pearls as he absorbed Maria's words. He threw his shoulders back and spoke resolutely. "In a few days there will be a statement that the Consul to Venezuela and General Hosada and his wife were all killed when an explosion occurred on the General's boat."

"And what about the Pearls? What about them?" Maria asked contemptuously.

Eduardo stared coldly at Bunny and Harriet before he spoke. "I've interrupted your social hour. Why not continue your leisure upstairs in the sitting room?" He stood, brandishing the gun at the Pearls. "Come with me," he said. "Maria, you're invited as well."

Inside the room, the three women heard the door lock behind them.

"Is there a way out of here?" Bunny asked Maria.

"None," she replied.

Bunny helped Harriet to the sofa. Harriet slumped against the cushions and groaned.

"Let me help you," Bunny said frantic with her concern. She lifted Harriet's legs and laid them gently on the sofa. From a carafe of water, she dampened a cloth and began to wipe the blood from Harriet's face. "Are you all right?" she cried.

"Yes," Harriet whispered, "can we help Maria?"

Grief-stricken and in shock, Maria sat stiffly in a

straight back chair. "The General is dead ... I cannot believe it. How could it happen?" She looked from Bunny to Harriet, the sorrowful expression on her face conveying the pain of her feelings, her disbelief.

Knowing it was futile to intrude on her grief, Harriet and Bunny sat quietly. For some time Maria was lost in thought, then she stood up.

"That fool has imprisoned us," she cried, "how dare he do this to Maria Hosada, First Lady of Los Pagos, wife of the General? And Turner dead ... murdered. Why?"

"We'll get the answers," Bunny said sympathetically, "I promise you."

Maria shook her head, closed her eyes. "And how will you do that?"

"We're going to get help—" Harriet began, trying to sit up.

"At this moment, USA, you need the help," Maria said, moving to her side. She sat on the edge of the sofa and began to open the buttons of the silk shirt now stained with blood and dirt.

"No," Harriet said, "don't."

"I won't hurt you," Maria said.

As she unbuttoned the shirt, Harriet raised her hands in protest.

"This isn't the time for modesty," Maria responded. "I know some first aid, let's see how badly you've been hurt."

Bunny made no attempt to stop Maria. The game was up anyway.

Harriet watched Maria's eyes widen as she took in the full view of the small, delicate breasts of a woman. Maria jerked her head around to stare at Bunny, a quizzical expression in her eyes; then very gently she placed the cloth she'd been holding in her hand onto Harriet's chest, and stood.

"Yes, I'm a woman," Harriet confirmed quietly.

"Maria shook her head, then smiled, then chuckled. "I knew you were a very special person, Harry Pearl," she said, winking as she knelt down to continue sponging Harriet's bruised and injured body. "Tell me what strange story brought this incredible business all about. It must be a most unusual tale."

When Harriet didn't answer, Bunny spoke. "We will tell you, but there are more surprises than the one you've just seen."

"You've given me fair warning," Maria said. "Now I want to hear your story from beginning to end."

Maria listened patiently as Bunny related all that had transpired from the first meeting in Stillwell's office to the present moment.

"Now you will hear my side," she said. "I did want Turner to help us find a source for the money. But you must understand what the Casino would mean to our impoverished island. Not for me or the General, God rest his soul, but for the people—for a better life. I want a hospital on Los Pagos. I want schools that teach our children possibilities for a new and better future. I want us to feel as if we are a part of *this* world—this century. And I, Maria Hosada, want to govern—fairly—but alone, not as the mistress of a man such as Alan Turner or the wife of a fool like Eduardo."

In an agitated voice, she said, "We must find a way to overpower that bear. I can assure you that you are in as much danger as I—"

"What kind of plan do you think he'll formulate?" Bunny asked.

"None," Maria replied with certainty. "He will act on impulse. He doesn't have much time to gather whatever support he might have built up in the General's Army, so he'll have to act alone."

Harriet moaned, "I don't know how much help I'll be."

Maria laughed at the sudden absurdity of her unmasked Prince Charming. "Harry Pearl, I'll always have a weak spot in my heart for you. Come on, Bunny," she said, "let's try to make this husband of yours a bit more comfortable. Help me find something to tape up Harry's rib cage."

"Harriet," the voice from the sofa responded weakly.

"Whatever you say, lover boy," Maria responded.

Stillwell watched Eduardo secure the General's craft to its mooring line, untie the dinghy and row back to the dock. There was no one visible on the deck of the boat. Something was amiss, he decided.

Eduardo walked hurriedly up the dock and toward the jeep. To Stillwell he looked agitated, perturbed, under heavy strain. Whatever Eduardo's problem, he'd be back soon enough. The best plan now was to see what developed here with Turner and the General.

Stillwell walked the length of the dock, thinking he'd surely see Turner or the General moving about on board. As if he were casually scanning the harbor, he took out his binoculars and gradually focused on the boat. The only discernible movments were caused by gulls feeding from a bait bucket. Whatever was going on below deck with the General and Turner, Stillwell thought, Eduardo would be right back.

Thirty minutes later he walked to his scooter. Nobody was on board. He would have seen one of them by now. What the hell was going on?

As he drove toward the Palace, Stillwell was buoyed by

a premonition, a confident feeling that the next few hours would provide him with all the opportunity he needed to break this case.

From his hillside lookout, he scanned the Palace grounds. It was nearly dusk, all was quiet.

Then he saw Eduardo leading Bunny, Harriet, and Maria Hosada toward the jeep. They were handcuffed to one another.

He laughed to himself. My super agents. Guarding the first lady.

Where could Eduardo be taking them, and why? What had happened to the General and Turner? Could they be dead? Could he be witnessing a coup? Was this the reason for the Russian guns, the mercenaries? Was a communist-backed foreign power trying to move into control at this very moment?

If Eduardo *had* indeed killed the General and Turner, then he was probably taking the three women to the yacht to get rid of them in the same way . . .

He can't march them down to the town dock handcuffed to one another, that's for goddamn sure, so where *are* they going?

The warehouse, he concluded, his confidence swelling over, where else? I'll beat them out there, be the official greeting party, what could be better? Then I'll get all the answers I need.

Concealed by foliage, Stillwell watched the jeep bounce down the dirt road near the airport. Eduardo leaped out a few feet short of the rustic wooden gate that guarded the road to the warehouse a quarter mile away. He hurried toward the gate, jumped over it and ran down the road, his figure disappearing in the dusk of twilight.

164

Stillwell turned his attention to the jeep. The women, still handcuffed to each other, were manacled to the jeep. Maria's left hand clutched the rollbar, her wrist securely handcuffed to it.

Stillwell watched while Harriet awkwardly moved over into the driver's seat. She's actually going to attempt to drive like that, he thought. That idiot Eduardo must have left the keys in the ignition.

Quickly, Stillwell stepped toward the jeep. "Going somewhere, ladies?" he inquired.

'What are *you* doing here?" Bunny asked in disbelief.

"I knew you two needed a helping hand," he sneered. "Looks like I didn't arrive a minute too soon—"

"Stillwell," Bunny interrupted, "can it, that guy's a nut. We've got to move!"

"If you girls *were* Senior Agent material, you wouldn't be in such a rush. I want to see what he's up to."

Stillwell stared ahead; night was falling fast. "Experienced surveillance," he boasted, "that's what's needed now. Before *I* make contact with the Agency, I want to confirm what's being stored in that warehouse. Munitions, I'm sure, but I want to know the size of that stockpile. Darkness is in my favor—I'll crawl up through the brush at the side of the road."

"You're going to need backup—cut us loose," Bunny pleaded. "He's gone over the edge, he's killed Turner—"

"Keep a lid on it, Silver. Pearl, tell your girlfriend to shut up. You two aren't the kind of backup I need," he said disgustedly. "You'll cause less trouble right where you are. I've been around long enough to recognize a military coup when I see one. I'll get the information you two should have had by now."

As he walked away from the jeep, he felt his prosthesis lock . . . but only for a second. Not now, he willed it, it can't happen now. Damn it, I can't risk crawling with this bum leg. He walked on, staying close to the brush and trees. There were no guards about, everyone appeared to be inside. He continued to move closer to the warehouse. He was almost there. Suddenly his prothesis locked, the shrill squeaking of it piercing through the usual night sounds.

The warehouse door swung open. The glare of the light within illuminated the silhouette of Lars Hansen and then Eduardo who stood in the doorway, gun in hand.

Lars leaped for the gun. "Don't shoot! We're too close to the ammo!"

Yet the shot rang out; Stillwell felt the bullet ricochet off his bad leg. He knew the next instant would be his last—it was all over. In his final seconds on this earth, the image he saw before him was not the warehouse but Bunny.

Harriet had found a pair of night binoculars in the glove compartment and she focused them in the direction of the distant warehouse. For a time, there was only the impenetrable darkness, then the warehouse door opened, she saw two or three figures in the light. Then Harriet saw the flame. "Down!" she screamed. "Get down!"

And then the explosion reached them.

In the coolness of twilight, Yarmi sat contentedly on her small veranda. She gazed across the lawn to the roof of her mistress's Palace, from which her own tiny cottage was only a short distance away.

She smiled as she looked at the basket of mangoes she had gathered earlier especially for her lady. She took a piece of the ripe fruit, held it in her strong hand, admired its shape and color. With her paring knife she cut the fruit in half, the seed clinging to the yellow flesh.

She had not seen her mistress all that afternoon. Where had she gone? She gripped the mango, squeezing the tender skin, feeling the juices run down her hand, over her wrist. The juice burned. She felt a chill run down her body. Suddenly she felt faint. She threw the mango to the ground and rushed from the cottage as fast as her large frame would allow.

As Yarmi hurried down the path toward the Palace, she saw shots of red and yellow flames burst across the distant sky.

"Maria," she cried, wringing her hands as she ran, "Maria!"

She rushed forward and found a guard. Staring at the smoke and flames that now filled the sky, he quickly helped Yarmi into his jeep and drove in the direction of the fire.

They weren't the first to arrive; several men and women had rushed to the scene on foot and were trying to lift the overturned jeep.

Yarmi rushed to a singed and blackened Bunny who, in shock, was helping the others.

"Go easy," Bunny cried, "there are two injured people under there."

"Maria?" Yarmi asked.

"Yes," Bunny said. "And Harry."

Yarmi bent down and put her shoulder to one of the wheels. With help from the crowd, the jeep was lifted and set right. Maria and Harriet lay sprawled on the damp earth, their handcuffs torn loose from the force of the explosion. Maria's handcuff was now a tattered bracelet encircling a wrist that was twisted backwards.

Yarmi, tears of relief in her eyes, knelt beside Maria.

She touched her gently. "Thank God you are alive. But, my lady, your wrist is surely broken. You may have other injuries as well," she said with concern.

"I'll be all right," she said in a shaky voice. "How are the others? Where are the Pearls?" Maria struggled to sit up.

Several feet away, Bunny sat next to Harriet, wiping her face with a cloth which had been passed to her by a woman in the crowd.

"I'm just so damn glad we're alive," Bunny said. "If Eduardo had driven that jeep much closer to the warehouse, we'd have all been blown sky-high."

"Don't talk that way," Harriet said in a pained voice as she clutched Bunny's hand.

"I can't help it, I don't want to lose you. We could have died because of that fucking Stillwell."

"But we didn't, Bunny. We're here and so is Maria. Try to calm yourself, you're in shock."

"I'm not," she said angrily. "You're the one who's hurt. And Maria. I'm *fine*."

"Bunny," Harriet said softly, "come here."

Harriet reached up for Bunny, opening her bruised arms as best she could. Bunny fell gently upon Harriet's breast and Harriet held her tightly, whispering assurances and endearments.

They were soon taken back to the Palace. Bunny was given a mild sedative. Harry was warned to favor his lacerated leg for the next few weeks, and Maria's broken wrist was set in a cast.

Before going to sleep that night, Maria comforted Yarmi, her good arm wrapped tightly around the older woman's waist, while Yarmi told her of her fears that evening.

"By now I should know to always trust your feelings," Maria said. "You tried to warn me of danger some time ago."

"Yes, I told you what I felt, but I had no vision of all that was about to happen. This is such a sorrowful time for you, mistress," Yarmi said sadly. "At least Eduardo will no longer cloud your dreams and for that I feel at peace. I no longer sense the presence of evil—"

"Then all has worked out for the best, hasn't it?" Maria asked with a broad smile for her trusted friend.

A week later, Bunny and Maria sat comfortably on the sunporch, wine glasses in their hands. They waited for Harriet who still found it a bit difficult to get about. She and Bunny would be leaving later that afternoon on a United States government plane.

Bunny gazed at an entirely new Maria. She wore a muted flowered dress and native sandals. Her hair was brushed back from her face, tortoise shell combs held it in place on the sides. She wore no makeup and her skin glowed with freshness.

"You like my new image," she said to Bunny with a mischievous smile.

"You look wonderful ... peaceful, lovely, in spite of all that has happened. Tell me your secret."

"No," Maria replied coyly, "we share too many now."

"That we do, Maria. I can't believe what's been going on around here the past few days. I never thought the Agency would come in so quickly to settle matters and we'd be on our way home so fast."

"You aren't sorry about that, are you? Once I informed your Mr. Perry that from now on Los Pagos would hold free elections, I could have had anything I wanted from that Agency—and that country—of yours. We *will* have a free election. Next month. Others may oppose me, but I have faith that I will be elected President."

"I wish we were going to be here to see it happen," Bunny replied with admiration.

"Why don't you stay and help with the campaign?"

"I don't think Sam Perry would see that as part of the job, Maria."

"Not even for two of his trusted *senior* agents? Those promotions you've so long desired are assuredly yours now, aren't they?"

"Damn right," Bunny said gleefully. "But for now all we really want to do is to get home and begin living our own lives . . . together."

"I toast that," Maria said simply, raising her glass.

"Then we'll try to lose ourselves in the next assignment. That's probably just as well . . . for us it's important that any unfavorable publicity be avoided. Can you just see the lurid headlines in the American papers?"

"It would be a field day for your journalists," Maria said laughing, "but don't worry, your secret's safe with me."

"What's going on?" Harriet asked as she walked stiffly down the stairs. "It sounds as if you two are having a party."

"Why shouldn't we be?" Bunny replied, grateful that they were recovering from their injuries so quickly. What a difference from the terrifying events of last week.

The days since then had passed so quickly. General Hosada had been buried with the full military honors he rightly deserved. For Stillwell, Hansen and Eduardo, a mass

170

was said where the warehouse once stood. Alan Turner's body had been flown back to the United States for a private family funeral.

"Come here, USA," Maria said softly, "let's take a good look at you."

Smiling, Harriet limped toward them. She wore blue linen trousers, a pink shirt and loafers. Her hair had been combed back from her face.

"Do you approve?" she asked Maria.

"Oh, yes, you look quite . . . handsome."

"Bunny, agree?"

"You're all right . . . USA," Bunny replied.

Then Harriet noticed that Bunny was wearing silver dangling earrings she'd not seen before. "Something new?" she asked, stepping forward to touch one of the earrings. "They're lovely."

"Ah," Maria said, "those are my going away gift to Bunny. For you Harry Pearl, I have a memento of the General's, his ivory walking stick. No doubt you will find it useful right now."

"Yes, I will," she said, looking at the details of the design. "It's so beautifully carved, thank you, Maria. This will always hold special memories for me . . . for us."

"Wonderful, USA. And now that you know our lovely island, you must come back when the resort is finished. As a democracy, we'll have our pick of investors, I can assure you. And who knows," she said, a smile dancing across her eyes, "maybe one day I'll find a man just like yours, Bunny."

With that, she reached over to Bunny; her fingers gently touched the silver earrings and a lovely chime filled the air.

A few of the publications of
THE NAIAD PRESS, INC.
P.O. Box 10543 • Tallahassee, Florida 32302
Phone (904) 539-9322
Mail orders welcome. Please include 15% postage.

MAGDALENA by Sarah Aldridge. 352 pp. Epic Lesbian novel
set on three continents.   ISBN 0-930044-99-1 $8.95

MURDER AT THE NIGHTWOOD BAR by Katherine V.
Forrest. 240 pp. A Kate Delafield mystery. Second in a series.
                                       ISBN 0-930044-92-4   8.95

ZOE'S BOOK by Gail Pass. 224 pp. Passionate, obsessive love
story.   ISBN 0-930044-95-9   7.95

WINGED DANCER by Camarin Grae. 228 pp. Erotic Lesbian
adventure story.   ISBN 0-930044-88-6   8.95

PAZ by Camarin Grae. 336 pp. Romantic Lesbian adventurer
with the power to change the world.   ISBN 0-930044-89-4   8.95

SOUL SNATCHER by Camarin Grae. 224 pp. A puzzle, an
adventure, a mystery—Lesbian romance. ISBN 0-930044-90-8   8.95

THE LOVE OF GOOD WOMEN by Isabel Miller. 224 pp.
Long-awaited new novel by the author of the beloved *Patience
and Sarah.*   ISBN 0-930044-81-9   8.95

THE HOUSE AT PELHAM FALLS by Brenda Weathers. 240
pp. Suspenseful Lesbian ghost story.   ISBN 0-930044-79-7   7.95

HOME IN YOUR HANDS by Lee Lynch. 240 pp. More stories
from the author of *Old Dyke Tales.*   ISBN 0-930044-80-0   7.95

SURPLUS by Sylvia Stevenson. 342 pp. A classic early
Lesbian novel.   ISBN 0-930044-78-9   7.95

PEMBROKE PARK by Michelle Martin. 256 pp. Derring-do
and daring romance in Regency England. ISBN 0-930044-77-0   7.95

THE LONG TRAIL by Penny Hayes. 248 pp. Vivid adventures
of two women in love in the old west. ISBN 0-930044-76-2   8.95

HORIZON OF THE HEART by Shelley Smith. 192 pp. Hot
romance in summertime New England.   ISBN 0-930044-75-4   7.95

AN EMERGENCE OF GREEN by Katherine V. Forrest. 288
pp. Powerful novel of sexual discovery. ISBN 0-930044-69-X   8.95

DESERT OF THE HEART by Jane Rule. 224 pp. A classic;
basis for the movie *Desert Hearts.*   ISBN 0-930044-73-8   7.95

These are just a few of the many Naiad Press titles—we are the oldest
and largest lesbian/feminist publishing company in the world. Please
request a complete catalog. We offer personal service; we encourage and
welcome direct mail orders from individuals who have limited access to
bookstores carrying our publications.